WARNING

This book contains sexually explicit scenes and adult language. It may be considered offensive to some readers. This book is for sale to adults ONLY.

* * * * * * * * * * * * * * * *

Please store your files wisely where they cannot be accessed by underage readers.

ISBN-13: 978-1987863789
ISBN-10: 198786378X

Other Books by Darla Dunbar:

<u>Romeo Alpha Blood Lines Romance Series </u>(This series follows "<u>The Romeo Alpha BBW Paranormal Shifter Romance Series</u>")

Twenty-four years have passed in relative peace for Amanda and Romeo. They've raised five children into adulthood and are thoroughly enjoying their lives as the Alpha King and Queen of the werewolves. At twenty-four, Sarina is just stepping into her powers and will be ripe for mating when her birthday comes in two weeks. What no one knows is the danger that lurks just outside their tight knit community. Romeo has made peace with the other clans and has enjoyed that peace, but it will all come crashing down around him when his oldest daughter comes of age to take a mate.

<u>The Alpha Feud BBW Paranormal Shifter Romance Series</u>

Eliza's life consisted of reporting on boring, crowd-pleasing events, like their country livestock fair. With the arrival of two handsome brothers, the lives of Eliza and her best friend, Melissa, are shaken to the core. For Eliza, the arrival of this new man becomes a test of her relationship with her current boyfriend, who she's been happily living with for over six years. Does Hayden, a complete stranger, really wield the power to make Eliza reconsider her relationship with Andrew?

<u>The Alpha Packed BBW Paranormal Shifter Romance Series</u>

Darlene has led a quiet life since suffering through a terrible break-up. She wants nothing more than to spend her time in front of the TV, away from any sort of trouble. But all that goes down the drain when handsome, rugged and rough Idris comes into her life. He is a werewolf on the lookout for his missing pack leader. Darlene quickly finds herself pulled towards this mysterious man and at the same time finds herself falling deeper and deeper into the world of the supernatural.

<u>The Daemon Paranormal Romance Chronicles</u>

The daemon infighting can only be stopped when a strong leader emerges to calm the different factions. Juno appears to be at the heart of the conflict. Things become complicated when Phoebe and Supay try to negotiate with the siren, Juno. The love triangle among Phoebe, Supay and Apollo become tense when Juno's meddling threatens to destroy any romance that develops.

<u>The Mind Talker Paranormal Romance Series</u>

Ananda finds herself on the run and she's not alone. With help from Jared, a stranger that she just met, the two evade capture by an organization that is intent on hunting her kind. Ananda and Jared are able to read minds. When an unfortunate incident happened involving a disturbed individual that resulted in the death of his schoolmates, the secret organization decided to take action.

<u>The Leather Satchel Paranormal Romance Series</u>

Valtina is stuck in Middle World, unable to pass on to The Afterlife. In order to redeem herself from past deeds done, she must help bring romance back into the world and stop The Dark Side from destroying love in its entirety. Following orders issued by Ladaya and armed with a leather satchel filled with the appropriate tools and weapons, Valtina embraces each mission with enthusiasm.

Get the latest update on new releases from the author at:

https://darladunbar.com/newsletter/

This book is Part Four of the "The Romeo Alpha BBW Paranormal Shifter Romance Series"

Book 1

Amanda Walker thinks that she has a normal and boring life. That is until after her 24th birthday. Everything changes when she meets the man who says he is supposed to be her husband. Denying everything the man says, she fights him every step of the way. But after he kidnaps her, Amanda discovers that there are some things about her family that her parents kept a secret all these years. Among the history of the family, she learns secrets she thought only happened in story books. Can Amanda tell the difference between truth and lies or does she hold the key to a mysterious legacy?

Book 2

After finally finding out who she really is, Amanda is ecstatic with her new life. Everything, however, is about to change. When a fire breaks out among the wolves, all suspicion is pointed towards her brother. Being forced to make the biggest choice of her life, Amanda must decide if being with Romeo is really where she should be or if her destiny lies elsewhere. Will she take the plunge that her heart is pushing her towards or will she do what is expected of her? Time can only tell.

Book 3

Now that Amanda is separated from her new husband and the other Radiants, she must go on a journey to

discover the power inside of her to defeat her evil
brother, Dean. She discovers the deep rooted history of
her kind as the lines between good and evil blur when
her sister-in-law begins to fall for the enemy. To
compound the situation, there is a surprise pregnancy
that is endangered from the escalating conflict between
Amanda and her brother.

Book 4

Coming off the death of her evil brother, Amanda still
feels anxious. She feels that the Radiants should stick
around in case Lilith decides to make an appearance.
When a woman shows up claiming to know Penelope
as well as Amanda's family, it seems almost too good to
be true. The spirit of Amanda's aunt shows up with a
warning that confirms her suspicions. The new guest
has a deadly secret that will lead to devastating
consequences. Will Amanda get her happy ending, or
will she lose the family she has worked so hard to
build?

A BBW Paranormal Shifter Romance Series

Romeo Alpha

Book Four

By Darla Dunbar

Table of Contents

Chapter One

AMANDA FELT like she had just been hit by a ton of bricks. Her husband Romeo and his twin brother Damon had been on the outs because of Elena, the witch who had tried to use dark magic to lure Romeo to her. Elena had torn Romeo's family apart and was supposed to be dead by Romeo's hand. Yet here she was, standing in front of them.

"I thought I killed you," Romeo said sternly, narrowing his eyes at Elena.

Amanda couldn't help but notice that the woman was incredibly beautiful; thin like a super model with long, flowing hair the color of redwood. But there was also something about her that reminded Amanda of a cat. Her movements and eyes looked feline.

"You almost did, but I'm pretty resilient. Sorry about my companion's behavior." Her words came out airy and wispy like her voice was being carried on the wind a long way. "Harming you, kidnapping you, was never my intention."

Elena approached Remus' body, and Audri glared up at her, encircling him with her arms for protection. Elena ran her fingers over his cold cheek and stood back up straight. "What a shame. I'm afraid either side he was on would have been a losing one for him. Dean never has been very forgiving. Well, I can see I've kept you a while, and I know you must be dying to get back to your little cubs."

Amanda gripped Romeo's arm so hard she felt she might break his bones. "What do you know of them?" she asked through gritted teeth. She was ready with her power, waiting for the moment to strike. She didn't like the way Elena had miraculously come back to life, how she had sucked the power from a dead man, or how she was looking at all of them like prey now.

"No need to fear me. I can simply feel that you have given birth recently. And since I don't see the little ones, I would assume that they are hidden somewhere safe. That was very smart of you. Dean surely would have used them against you."

Amanda was sure she heard a threat hidden under that statement, but she said nothing. She was ready to go home.

"I'll be seeing you." Elena turned and walked away slowly, leaving all of them in shock.

"Amanda?" Penelope stepped forward to embrace her.

Amanda suddenly felt something in herself let go, and she began to cry. They were reunited, finally, all of the Radiants and their daughters.

"I'm so glad you're all right," she whispered through tears as the rest of the Radiants stepped forward.

"Amanda, I must stay behind for a while and let my family see that I am all right. I will be to your home soon to continue our training. Would you mind taking my daughter with you? I will send Alessandra with you as well." Catrona looked at her with a soft smile. Even after being trapped in a crystal for months, she still exuded so much confidence and beauty.

"It would be my honor," Amanda replied, taking Catrona's daughter's hand. Amanda closed her eyes and felt the power running through her. Her time with Ariella ensured that she knew all there was to know, perhaps even more than Penelope did, about being a Radiant. She couldn't wait to tell Penelope all about her time in Faerie.

She felt the Earth and the ley lines, all the energy the Earth provided her, and she willed all of them home.

November 7, 2014

I am happy to say that Romeo and I are finally back at the estate for good. The repairs are all finished, and though we lost much of the furniture and the downstairs, the library room with the diaries, and my bedroom are miraculously still intact. Sometimes, I think there must be someone watching over me. I'd like to think it's my parents or maybe even my aunt. I reread her diary from time to time and talk with others about what she was like. I see more and more of her in myself each passing day. She was such a strong and loving woman. I wish I could have known her.

As far as Elena, or Lilith, or whatever the witch's name is, everything has been rather quiet on that front. It may be the calm before the storm, but I have enjoyed the time of peace to spend time with my new husband and my two beautiful children. They look like the perfect mix of both Romeo and I, and I am so proud. They are already learning to sit up and are cooing and laughing. It brings more joy to my life than I ever could have imagined.

However, there are other issues to address. Today is going to be a big day. The Radiants are having a meeting to decide whether or not they should all stay here any longer. Our powers are starting to cause many disturbances in the weather and the environment, just like they warned me it would. But I still feel uneasy with them going. I can feel something brewing, and it's coming soon. Hopefully, I can keep them from leaving just a little while longer.

Tonight, we are also holding a formal ceremony to honor both Damon's and Remus' life. Not everyone agrees with it, but I thought everyone deserved a time to grieve, and both men deserved to be remembered. Remus died to save Audri's life. Even if he was only a good man for that last ten seconds of his existence, it's enough to say he changed. It's that simple.

Until my next thoughts, I bid adieu.

As Amanda closed the leather-bound book, the ground began to shake, and she could hear the kitchenware rattling in the cabinets.

"Get Jason to the door frame!" she called out to whoever might get to him in time as she scooped Sarina up in her arms and placed herself in the doorway. It was just one of the many earthquakes that had plagued the town lately, and they were getting worse, spreading over a further area. Amanda had become afraid to turn on the news because the center of the earthquake would always be nearby, and she didn't want to hear about it. She wasn't ready to admit fault.

Soon, the quaking stopped, and she rushed into the family room to find Audri holding Jason and soothing his crying. It turned out that her little boy was the fussy one while Sarina was always calm and collected. She kissed both babies on the head and wondered if Romeo was all right. He had been at his father's house for a guy's night and was supposed to be headed back home that morning. She and Audri had been spending time together, talking about boys; those boys being the late Remus and Benjamin.

Audri and Benjamin had just begun repairing their relationship. She had tried to explain herself right after they got home, but Benjamin hadn't been very kind about it then. Lately, he had become more understanding, probably because he missed her. Not that it mattered what his reasons were, because Amanda knew Audri needed him and still wanted him. It made Amanda think of the balance in the world, much like with magic.

There had been two men on Earth for Audri to love, but she'd only had a short time with one of them. Then, he passed. Now there was only one man for Audri, like it should be. No matter how terrible that sounded or how hard it had been to lose Remus, it was necessary.

"Have you talked to Romeo?" Audri asked out of the blue, setting Jason down on his play gym. Amanda narrowed her eyes, wondering what Audri really wanted to know. She was clearly fishing for something.

"No, but he should be back any moment. I hope nothing bad happened because of the earthquake. But why are you concerned all of a sudden?"

Audri sighed and sat down on the floor with Jason. Amanda sat Sarina down with him, and she instantly began practicing rolling over. "I was just wondering if he had talked to Benjamin at all. I'm pretty sure he was supposed to be at Dad's last night with him. I just can't stand this whole thing; it's driving me crazy. It's even more awkward knowing that we're having that ceremony later tonight for Damon and Remus. I feel like it's going to throw us back into a big fight."

Amanda couldn't help but chuckle. It made her think of her own stubbornness over Romeo when she first arrived and found out what she was. Love was such a fickle thing. "Audri, I don't think that's going to happen. I don't know that yours and Benjamin's relationship will ever be the same, but I do know that you both love each other very much. I don't think there's anything stronger than that, so you'll be fine."

"I'm glad that you're so sure, but Benjamin is not Romeo."

"You're right, and that's probably a good thing. Romeo is a much less forgiving person, I'm sure." Amanda patted Audri on the back as she heard a familiar voice coming through the doorway.

"Amanda?"

When Romeo called her name, she ran to him, jumping instantly into his arms.

"I thought something may have happened to you. There was another earthquake. Did you feel it?"

"Yes," Romeo answered, giving Amanda a kiss on the lips and setting her down in front of him. "I don't think it was that strong, but it stopped traffic for a moment. I don't really think it caused any damage." Romeo seemed to be sugar coating it, something he had gotten good at over the last few weeks. Amanda was beginning to see right through it, though.

"You're doing it again," she whispered, feeling her brow crease with worry. She knew for a fact that the earthquakes had already caused some damage around town, knocking down some older buildings and putting some cracks in the roads. No one had gotten hurt yet, but she knew it was just a matter of time.

"I'm telling the truth. I didn't see any damage to anything, Amanda. You need to stop beating yourself up about this. They're here for everyone's safety and to teach their powers to the next generation. It's important that all four of you are involved. In the long run, it won't be that long that you're together. We'll just ride it out."

"Ugh, get a room, you two," Audri gagged, pulling some milk out of the fridge to make the bottles.

Romeo, as if just remembering he had children, got wide eyes and then ran to where the babies were playing. His overprotectiveness had recently extended to them as well. "I can't believe you left them in here alone."

Audri rolled her eyes at Amanda as Romeo said it. Amanda tried not to laugh. It was very sweet, really.

"So, how is Benjamin?" Audri dared to ask, trying to sound nonchalant, but failing miserably.

Romeo shrugged. "He's fine, why?" The girls rolled their eyes at each other. It was useless talking to boys about matters of the heart. They just didn't understand.

"Just curious." Audri let it go and brought the bottles of milk into the living room where she handed one to Romeo. "Here, feed your son. It's my turn to feed Sarina, and it's Amanda's turn to rest. She was up all night pumping this stuff so that it would be ready."

Amanda nodded and smiled. Everyone had been so helpful with the babies to make sure that she and Romeo didn't have to lose as much sleep, but she still had to pump a lot. The babies didn't seem to like feeding directly off of her, and to be honest, she thought it was a little strange as well.

Amanda was about to head to the bedroom when the door flew open. In came the other three Radiants along with the two young women learning to take over. It was time for the meeting, apparently, and Amanda instantly felt exhausted. Was she ready to fight for them to stay? Would they even take her concerns into account?

"Let us find somewhere to convene," Catrona announced, sounding official. The two younger girls came to ooh and aww over the babies, apparently not being allowed to join in the discussion. Amanda followed the three women outside to the back, overlooking the mountains. Amanda just took in the scenery for a moment, savoring the fact that she was finally back home.

As usual, the Radiants formed a circle, and Penelope squeezed Amanda's hand a moment. They hadn't seen much of each other since getting back. Penelope had retreated with the Radiants, wanting to learn more. Plus, Amanda had a sneaking suspicion she wanted to stay away from Elijah as well. It was probably too painful to be around him, knowing they could never truly be together.

"As you all know, things have been affected by us all being together. This is what we have been warned about. There are too many of us in one place, and our combined power is affecting the Earth. Our time together has been important. We have defeated the darkness of Dean, and we have taught Penelope and our daughters the way of the Radiants. We must decide if there is any reason to risk staying here. Alessandra and

I can return home and continue the lessons for our daughters on our own, and Penelope can stay with Amanda to continue. Since Amanda has learned from the Queen of Faerie herself, I believe she is capable," Catrona said, giving Amanda a penetrating look.

Amanda nodded. She was happy that they were so confident in her, but she really needed an excuse for them to stay. She racked her brain for what to say when it was her turn to speak.

"It is my opinion that it is not worth the risk to stay with the information we have at the moment," Catrona continued. "But I would like to hear from each one of you what you think." She nodded over to Alessandra.

"I agree with Catrona. We came here for two reasons, and I believe we have accomplished them. Our being here is already affecting the environment. I don't believe it's fair to stay and continue to cause trouble for the locals, even as much as I enjoy being here with everyone." A tear escaped Alessandra's eye. She had talked about Amanda's mother constantly and seemed to enjoy reliving those memories. It was a sad thing that they ever had to leave. Why did it have to be such a bad thing to be together?

Catrona pointed to Penelope next. "I will agree with whatever the two senior members have decided. I do not feel that I have enough experience to make a true decision. I believe Catrona and Alessandra know best." Penelope stared straight ahead, not even blinking or flinching, but squeezed Amanda's hand again. She sounded defeated, as though all the light was gone from her.

"Very well, then. It seems our decision is made, but it wouldn't be fair not to hear from Amanda first," Catrona said, smiling around at them, sadly. As professional as she was, Amanda could tell she wasn't thrilled about leaving either. They must feel so lonely being so far away, being the only ones like them where they lived.

Amanda took a deep breath, deciding to tell the truth and see where it got her. "I absolutely respect your decision on the matter. I know I have not been one of you for very long, but I have to humbly disagree with the majority opinion."

Penelope looked at her, horrified, but Amanda wasn't about to not speak her mind when offered the chance. "I don't want to hurt people anymore, and it does scare me that these earthquakes are getting worse. However, what happened with Dean did not go as planned. The woman known as both Lilith and Elena was not who we thought she was, and she has absorbed a great deal of dark magic. I do not know what she intends to do with it, or if she means anyone harm. But I just have this feeling of foreboding that something is coming. And I fear if we split up, it will put everyone in even more danger. If we could just stay together a little while longer, we could ensure that the problem has been taken care of."

Alessandra raised her hand before speaking again. "I'd like to change my vote, Catrona. A Radiant's intuition is much different from some human inkling or paranoia. She could be right, and then none of our efforts would have mattered. I don't think it will hurt to stay just a little bit longer to be sure."

"It seems we have a tie. Penelope, would you care to break it?" Catrona looked to Penelope, who looked frozen. Amanda rubbed her back to support and comfort her.

"I think they are right, Catrona, but the ultimate decision is up to you." It came out quick, in one breath.

"Then, I will allow six more weeks, and no more. The land cannot take any longer than that."

Amanda tried not to act too happy at the small victory, so she headed inside to find Romeo but was stopped by Penelope. "What is it, my friend?" she asked, worried about what might be going on with her.

"I wanted to ask how you were, how the family was. We haven't seen each other much." Penelope's gaze was trained on the ground.

"Well, I'm all right. Everyone's helping with Jason and Sarina, especially Aurora and Audri. The babies are just growing so fast, I can't believe it. It's like I blink and they've grown an inch or two. But I'm pretty sure the part of the family you really want to know about is Elijah." Amanda gauged Penelope's reaction as she looked around to see if anyone was within earshot. "He's all right, though I haven't seen a lot of him now that all the houses are rebuilt. He comes and visits along with Jeremiah once in a while. I think he was at the guys' night with Romeo last night. He might know more."

Penelope sighed, letting her shoulders sag. "Thanks, Amanda, but I should probably just let it go. Nothing good can come from our relationship, even if we're only friends. It hurts to be around him as well as to be away from him. I've thrown myself into this whole thing so that I'd be distracted, but it isn't even working. How will I ever get over him?"

Amanda embraced Penelope. "I'm not sure, but hopefully time will take care of it. I'm so sorry that this is happening to you. My choice was obvious because I was already in so deep with Romeo. We had mated and were engaged to be married. You don't have that sure relationship with Elijah. I'm here for you no matter what happens, okay?"

Penelope nodded as she pulled away, and Amanda went back into the house to find Romeo snoring on the couch. She gently shook his shoulder. "I guess the guys' night didn't include a lot of sleep," she whispered into his ear, but he suddenly startled, jumping up and looking around. His fists were clenched. "What's wrong, Romeo?" she asked, concerned. "You're scaring me."

He slowly relaxed and met her gaze. "Sorry, my love, it must have been a nightmare. I had one last night, too; that's why I'm so tired."

"Oh, I'm sorry. Why don't we let someone else watch the babies, and we can go take a nap before the ceremony tonight." She held out her hand, and he took it, walking up the stairs with her into the bedroom.

Chapter Two

Amanda snapped the red onesie onto Sarina and picked her up, holding her on the side of her hip. She looked over to see that Aurora was putting a cute blue outfit on Jason and smiled. "Lookin' good, little man," she said, looking down at her son. "Doesn't your little brother look so handsome?" She kissed Sarina on the forehead as Aurora picked up Jason and they all walked outside together.

Everyone else was already gathered outside. She could see the flicking flames from the bonfire they were building back near the mountains at the back of the property, far away from the house. The stars were all out, and it was a cool and clear night, perfect for the ceremony to honor the two fallen werewolves.

The women took their time getting to the bonfire, knowing that the babies wouldn't be able to stand the heat from the flames for long anyway. Aurora had volunteered to help so that Romeo could give a speech about his brother. Aurora insisted that she had made her peace with the fact that he was gone long ago, even though she appreciated his rescue of their sister. She also made it no secret that she did not like Remus, though she felt sympathy for her sister over losing any man she had feelings for.

As they approached, Romeo came up to her and wrapped his arm around her waist. Penelope and the other two Radiants headed over to her. "I didn't think you guys would be coming to this?" Amanda smiled at them inquisitively.

"Who do you think made this fire?" Catrona smiled, showing a rare side of herself as her daughter came up by her side. "Of course, she helped."

"And I'll be here for when it needs putting out," Alessandra laughed. Both women were in jeans and shirts, which was even stranger for Amanda. She was so used to seeing them looking so formal and perfect, but it was nice to see that they were involved in her life, supporting her family and their losses.

"I think I'm up first," Romeo whispered in her ear and then kissed her on the forehead. "After the speech, I'll come back and hold my daughter. I'd love to spend more time with her. I'm always ending up with Jason. You should spend some time with your son." He nodded over to where Aurora and Audri were standing, playing with Jason. He was right about that.

"That sounds nice, Romeo. I love your ideas, and I love you. I hope you know that. Be strong up there, all right?"

Romeo nodded, and she could see the determination in his eyes as he let go of her and looked out at the bonfire and all the people surrounding it. "Of course, to both those things. I love you, too. Thank you for being here for me."

"I wouldn't be anywhere else." She gave him a sweet smile before he walked away, causing the group to gather closer to the fire, some standing and some sitting. The impact just two lives could have on so many people was amazing.

"I want to start by thanking everyone for being here tonight, regardless of your feelings or relationship with my twin brother or the other man we are honoring here tonight. Lives are precious things. Even the life that we ended to save this world from darkness and to save this family, was important in the grand scheme of things."

Amanda felt tears welling up in her eyes. She had done a lot of thinking about the loss of the brother she never knew she had. She often thought that if they had met sooner that maybe his fate would have been different. Maybe they could have really been family.

"Damon was the perfect alpha; both strong and caring. It took me years to learn that compassion didn't make me weak as a leader. Damon knew that from the start. He was a fun guy to be around, to grow up with, always the life of the party. He always knew what to say or do to cheer his siblings up when they were down. In the end, his love and compassion became his downfall, but I don't think anyone should regret that part of him. It made him who he was. It was the woman who took advantage of him who should be at fault. I hope that wherever he is, he receives all of our love and forgiveness for everything that transpired. He will always be my brother; my twin. And I hope his spirit lives on in my own son, Jason. I will teach him to be strong and to care just like Damon did." Romeo bowed toward the fire and the group, and many heads dropped low in thought.

She had only known Damon for a matter of hours when he held her hostage for her brother. But she could see how he regretted the way he had acted, that there was a wonderful man under there. She wished she had gotten to know that guy. But then she would have probably had to marry him and not her Romeo. Fate knew what was best for her.

Romeo walked back over to her and took Sarina, so she went over to grab Jason, who was now being held by Audri. A few more people said a few words about Damon as they all stood there and enjoyed their now-sleeping babies.

"I think it's getting time to take them inside," she whispered to Romeo as Jeremiah finished talking about his son.

Romeo placed Jason in one arm and Sarina in the other. "I think you should stay here for Audri. I'll take them inside and watch them. I've made my peace." He kissed her on the forehead and ran their children back to the house. She watched his speed and grace as he disappeared into the night before turning back to Audri.

"Are you going to say something about your brother or Remus?" she asked.

Audri shrugged. "I'm nervous about it, and no one else has said anything about him, really. I'm scared of what they'll all think."

"Audri, this was supposed to be for him, too. If no one says anything, it's pointless. I'd say something if I knew him, but I didn't. Get up there. I'll be here for you afterward."

Audri nodded and made her way in front of the crowd, looking entirely unsure of herself. The family quieted again, watching her to see what she would do. Amanda could feel the tension, and Aurora and Benjamin both appeared by her side.

"She's going to talk about him, isn't she?" Benjamin asked her, looking like a little boy in the flickering firelight.

Amanda decided not to hold her tongue in this instance. Audri needed support.

"Yes, she is, and I hope you support her. She's so afraid of what you're going to think, what all of you think. She's doing what she feels is right, with no support from anyone. Isn't that how Damon ended up where he did, because his family abandoned him for his feelings? Please, don't do it. You don't have to understand, but you can't only love her when it's convenient."

Amanda saw that he was listening, taking what she was saying to heart. At least Audri would have someone on her side when all was said and done.

"Hello, everyone," Audri started, sounding timid. "First, I want to thank everyone for the kind words about my brother. He was a great brother, even in the end, when we had all shunned him. He saved me from a dangerous situation, cared about me even when I didn't care about him. I understand the position he was in now more than ever, now that I find myself in a similar one. I know a lot of you were not okay with what went on between us or that Remus is being honored alongside my brother tonight, but I believe he deserves honor as well. Remus was not always a good man. In fact, most of the time he was pretty bad, but there was a spark in him, something about him that pulled people in. The most important thing was that he spent his whole life loving me. He even once told me that was the only good quality he'd ever have. It doesn't sound like something a knight in shining armor would say, but in the end, that's what he was. He spent his last moments protecting me and my family, and for that I am eternally grateful. It is for that act and for our childhood together as friends that he deserves to be remembered tonight. It is that part of him that I will carry with me always."

Audri came back over to Amanda, sobbing. Amanda held her and rubbed her back like she was sure she'd do for Sarina one day. She gave Benjamin a hard look as a tense silence overtook the crowd. Clearly, no one was very happy about Remus' inclusion, and no one else wanted to speak of him.

As Benjamin made his way to the front, Amanda turned Audri around to show her, and they both froze, wondering exactly what he might do or say.

"Hey, everyone. I have a little story to tell. As you all know, we all grew up together, though I was the youngest of the group. I remember looking up to

Romeo and Remus and the rest of them like they were gods, and I was just this puny little cub wanting to play with the big boys. They used to all pick on me and push me into the mud and stuff." Amanda heard some laughs go around the crowd and clung to her sister-in-law. If this wasn't a romantic gesture, she wasn't sure what was.

"But there was this one time when I got hurt pretty bad. I actually broke my arm trying to do something they were doing, but I didn't want to cry in front of them. So, I was left alone, unable to move, when Remus came back for me. He showed me how to pop my arm back in place and sat with me while I healed. Then, he made it look like we had been fighting so that the guys would think that's why we had stayed behind. It was probably the only time we were friendly with each other, but that was the big surprise of Remus. Every once in a while, he would come out and do something so amazing it would redeem every bad thing he'd ever done. The same is true of what he did with Audri. I know that he has caused some trouble in the past, and there's no way to sugar coat it or forget it. But he saved the woman I love. I can't hate him for that. I have to thank him. So, let's all raise our glasses to Remus."

Many people grabbed beers or whatever they were drinking and held them up in tribute as Benjamin walked away. "Go to him," she told Audri, knowing she couldn't allow the moment to pass.

Audri threw herself at him, forcing him to catch her, and she planted her lips against his. Amanda could practically see sparks flying through the air around them. She smiled to herself and decided it was time to head back inside with her husband and children. Her work was done.

<<<>>>

"How are they doing?" she asked, approaching Romeo on the couch. He had one baby in each arm, and they were fast asleep. Unfortunately, Romeo was asleep as well, but she could tell by the expressions on his face and his jerky movements that he was having another one of his bad dreams. That would be the third one. Dark circles were starting to form under his eyes from lack of proper sleep, and she was becoming worried. Was he so stressed out and hurt over the death of his brother that it was taking over his sleep and dreams?

She carefully picked up Sarina and carried her up to the bedroom to place her in the bassinet that she was starting to get too big for. They would have to go get cribs for them to sleep in and find them a room in the house. She hadn't done it yet because she was dreading not having them with her at night. But she knew it was best for their development to learn to self soothe and all that.

On her way back down the stairs, she heard an awful growl coming from her husband and then a blood-curdling scream from Jason. She ran down the stairs to see that Romeo had jumped up again and started looking around. Jason had woken up in his arms and was red-faced and upset about being woken up so abruptly. She quickly scooped him out of Romeo's grasp and tried to get her husband's attention. It was like he was in some kind of trance.

Finally, recognition came to his face, and he looked white as a sheet.

"You had another dream, didn't you?" she asked sympathetically. He only nodded and headed upstairs.

"I'll be up there as soon as I get Jason back to sleep so I can put him down," she called after him, but there was no response. That feeling in her gut was getting worse, making her feel sick again. Something told her that her husband was suffering from something bad, but she didn't know what. Maybe she should talk to Jeremiah, see if he could help him out at all. He couldn't keep going on like that with no rest.

She began walking around the floor and singing softly into Jason's ear until he quieted down and closed his eyes. She had a feeling Jason was going to be real fun when he got older. He was already a yeller. She laughed to herself at the thought and headed up the stairs to her bedroom and found Romeo passed out on the bed already, his clothes laying in a pile at the foot of the bed. Maybe all he needed was to be comfortable.

She placed Jason in his own bassinet and laid down herself next to her snoring husband. She ran her hands over his warm skin and thought about how lucky she was to have been chosen to be his wife. Anyone in the world could have mated with him and had his beautiful children, but it was Amanda, the ordinary brown-haired orphan who loved animals, who became his lucky wife and mate.

She fell asleep next to him and dreamed of her children and her amazing husband.

Next to her, Romeo dreamed of a witch, a very evil and powerful witch, who wanted to use him for her evil plans. For she was the first witch to ever dabble in dark magic, and she wanted to finish what she started many hundreds of years earlier. This was the dream that Romeo dreamed every time he fell asleep, and he always woke up, feeling her presence, the hair prickling on his neck.

A few hours later, Amanda woke up to find Romeo writhing next to her, practically throwing himself off the bed. The clock told her that it was after three in the morning, and both of the babies were still sound asleep.

"Romeo, Romeo!" She tried to be quiet as he thrashed around. She needed to wake him up. Finally, she rolled him onto his back and opened his eyes but had to stifle a scream when the whites of his eyes were all that was showing. His eyeballs had rolled up into his head, and he began practically seizing.

Not knowing what else to do, she placed her hand against his chest and closed her eyes, drawing her power around her. She pulled all the life inside of him and from in their home and used the power to calm his body. He finally stopped seizing and fell back into a deep, dreamless sleep, but he was drenched with sweat.

Amanda's night had already been ruined, so she tiptoed down the hall to find where Penelope was sleeping, hoping she would have some advice on how to help Romeo. But Penelope was nowhere to be found, and she found herself worrying about two people now as she made her way back to her own bedroom where she stared at the ceiling for the rest of the night.

Chapter Three

"Do you remember anything about last night?" Amanda asked Romeo as he helped her prepare breakfast for everyone. Penelope had showed up early in the morning and was watching both Jason and Sarina while they played host to those who had stayed over after the bonfire. That included Jeremiah, the Radiants and their daughters, and Aurora. Benjamin and Audri had apparently disappeared shortly after the story he told about Remus. Amanda hoped they had gone somewhere to make up, especially considering a full moon was coming up. Maybe she'd get to finally attend their wedding.

"Not really, other than I had a nightmare again. I can never remember what they're about though, once I'm fully awake."

Amanda looked him up and down with concern and gave him an embrace from the side. "I was thinking about talking to Catrona or Alessandra today to see what they thought about what's going on with you. You seemed like you had a seizure and were sweating, and your eyes rolled back into your skull. I had to use my magic to calm you down. I was so worried about you."

"It's probably just about my brother. I lost my twin, and I must be having a harder time getting over it than I thought. Don't make a big fuss about it. It'll pass."

"I'm not so sure. I have a bad feeling about this, Romeo. It was scary."

"I said, I don't want to make a big deal out of it. That's final!" He walked out of the house with a slam of the door and Jason started crying in the other room. Amanda shook her head and went to plate all the food as people started coming down the stairs, probably woken up by the smell of bacon. His behavior was just more proof to her that it was something to be concerned about, and she planned on talking to someone whether he liked it or not. He was becoming irritable and so tired. She couldn't let it keep going.

As she began setting everyone's plates down on the table, a knock came at the door. She wondered who it could be. Audri and Benjamin didn't tend to ask any permission before just barging in. So, she headed to the door and opened it to find a plain-looking woman standing there with straight dirty blond hair and a wool coat on with some boots.

"Amanda, is that you?" the woman asked with a genuine-looking smile.

"I'm sorry, but should I know you?" Amanda asked, feeling a little confused and suspicious.

"No, I would guess not. I haven't seen you since you were just a baby. I was only maybe twelve or thirteen myself at the time. My name is Nancy Santos. My mother knew your mother."

Amanda froze in the doorway, wondering how in the world she had missed this person with all the reunions that had already happened. No one had even mentioned her before. Penelope came up by her side and looked just as shocked before giving the woman a hug.

"Penelope! I would recognize you anywhere."

"So you somehow knew Penelope and my mother?" Amanda questioned, feeling totally out of the loop.

"I only met you the once. I know that your parents left shortly afterward, your mother wanting to get away from her family. But I grew up with Penelope until we moved away to England. When her parents let her play outside, she would follow me around like a lost puppy dog." The woman laughed, and Amanda opened the door to let her in.

"How did you know where to find me?" Penelope asked with a huge smile on her face. It was the first truly happy emotion Penelope had expressed in a long time. Amanda may not know the woman, but she had to let her stay a while if she was making Penelope so happy. Besides, she was always excited to learn more about her mother.

"Well, I actually came back in town and all and went looking for you. I found out that your father had passed and was told this crazy story when I tried asking around about you. The witch community seems to have really dwindled. So, anyway, I'm a bit embarrassed to admit using my powers like this, but I actually did a little locator spell and then realized whose estate this was. I knew it couldn't be a coincidence, so I came right out and here you both are. I'm so excited you found each other."

Amanda smiled politely and looked the woman up and down. Nancy looked so plain, almost like a bag lady, but she was talking like some sorority girl. She had to be the most interesting person Amanda had ever seen.

"Yes, we did. Though, the circumstances weren't the best, we're together now. She's actually a Radiant, like me," Penelope explained.

"Oh, wow, that's great. So, both your mothers gave you guys their powers, then? It sounds like you must be close. Anyway, I don't want to keep you, but I heard about the both of you losing your families and thought that you could use a friend or even some information. Amanda's mother was a secretive one, for sure."

Amanda nodded in agreement. Her mother had hidden being a powerful witch and Radiant from her as well as another child. There was no telling what else there was to know.

"Well, I'd love to hear stories about my family. It turns out they kept a lot from me and then died before they could tell me anything. Filling in the gaps would make you my new best friend. How about you stay for a while? As you can imagine, I have plenty of spare bedrooms," Amanda offered, sitting down with the two of them on the couch.

"I don't know, it looks like you have a full house already. I don't want to be in the way," Nancy responded as she looked around the house.

Amanda realized what she must be seeing. She did have a full house with everyone eating breakfast and the babies being passed around from person to person. Even Romeo had walked back in, making it even more crowded. Not that it mattered, since the estate was impossibly huge, but it might seem intimidating to a witch in a house full of werewolves and Radiants.

"Oh, they're mostly family and some friends. We had a sort of ceremony last night for some family members we lost recently. It's mostly just Romeo and I and sometimes Penelope and the other Radiants."

"Oh, I'm so sorry for your loss. But did you say the other Radiants? You mean, they're actually all here?" Nancy started craning her neck and looking around the corner into the dining room to see. It was like Amanda had just told her that Johnny Depp was in her house.

"Yes." Penelope laughed as she said it. "They have been staying here teaching us their ways."

"Wow, that's amazing. Sounds like I've missed a lot. Well, I was really looking forward to seeing you both and talking about the past, so I think I'll take you up on your offer, Amanda." Nancy smiled up at Amanda, and Amanda wondered if she'd changed her tune because of the Radiants. Either way, she was going to get to learn more about her mother.

"I'll help her find a room. You go take care of those babies," Penelope offered, leading Nancy up the stairs.

Romeo appeared by her side. "I'm sorry for my behavior. I don't know what's going on with me."

"It's all right," she told him, giving him a quick squeeze. She couldn't ever really stay mad at him.

"So, who is that I saw going up the stairs with Penelope?"

"Her name is Nancy. She's a witch who grew up with Penelope. She said that her mother and my mother were friends and that she met me once as a baby before my parents ran with me. She's here to visit from England. She wants to tell me more about my mother, so I'm letting her stay here. I hope that's okay?" She looked up at her husband hopefully.

"It's fine, honey. This is your estate, so it's your decision."

"You're my husband; it's our estate." She smiled warmly up at him and stood up on her tiptoes to give him a peck on the cheek, and he slapped her on the ass.

She giggled but then heard the babies crying from whoever's arms they were in. "It must be time for another feeding." She squeezed his hand and went to grab them, reminded once again of her new status as a mother; one she wouldn't give up for anything.

As she passed the stairs a cold chill ran through her body, and she swore she heard her name whispered even though no one was there. Maybe she needed some sleep just as badly as Romeo.

<<<>>>

"I bet they're all wondering where we are. We should probably get back," Audri said, concerned and sitting up from where she was on the bed. The blanket slid off her to show her small breasts and flat stomach. Benjamin ran his hand up and down her back, which sent ripples throughout her body. She'd forgotten what it was like to be with him like that. His touch was intoxicating.

"I'm pretty sure they know where we are and what we're doing, Audri." Benjamin slid across the bed and sat behind her, wrapping his legs around her. She could feel his soft shaft pressing up against her backside and starting to respond to the touch of their bare bodies.

She let her hair fall to one side, and Benjamin took the invitation to kiss and nibble down her neck and shoulder. His hands came around front to hold her breasts; one in each hand, and he began to massage them gently. Her head rolled forward, relaxed, as she began to moan softly.

"Stay here with me," he whispered into her ear. He was certainly driving a hard bargain.

Audri tried to protest as he pulled her back onto the bed, exposing the rest of her body to him. But as his hand ran down her thigh and to her clit, she couldn't resist anymore.

The ceremony was over, and he was probably right that Amanda knew where she was and would tell her to stay with him anyway. She couldn't believe how easy it had suddenly become for them after so much tension for so long. She had been sure he was done with her the moment she couldn't call what happened with Remus a mistake, but it turned out that Amanda was right all along; Benjamin loved her no matter what.

His thumb began to make wide circles on her clit, and it began to swell as her center got wet. It was too bad it wasn't time to mate yet, because she'd willingly do it, no longer feeling the need to wait for wedding bells. There wasn't anyone else alive she wanted that experience with.

She moaned and reached for him as his fingers slipped farther down, feeling around inside of her. She was dripping all over him as his fingers slid in an out with precision, and she began to rock her hips into him, loving the feel of it.

Her legs began to shake as she climaxed. She moaned and quaked under his touch. She found Benjamin's swollen member and began teasing it with the tips of her fingers. His back arched, and he closed his eyes in response to her gentle touch. She took the opportunity to surprise him, climbing on top of him and lowering herself over his hard shaft.

His eyes flew open in shock, and a gasp escaped his throat. She let out a pleasure-filled sigh as he was finally completely in, and then she began rocking back and forth slowly, her hair brushing his stomach. Benjamin held her hips and began doing the work for her, shaking her body around like a rag doll. Her breasts made a slapping noise as they bounced up and down with the quick movement he was forcing her body to make.

She screamed his name as he slammed in and out of her, hitting every spot inside of her and stretching her to her limit. She looked down into his eyes and saw how he worshipped her body and how his brow was dripping with sweat from the effort. She leaned down so that her nipples were touching his chest, and she kissed him passionately on the lips. He moaned into her mouth, and she could feel he was holding himself back, ready to explode at any moment.

Audri squeezed her muscles around his shaft, helping her orgasm along as it finally came. The pulsing forced him to climax as well, gushing inside of her like a geyser.

Chapter Four

Amanda felt a chill as she tiptoed from her bedroom. She had heard that whisper of her name again and couldn't sleep, especially since Romeo was thrashing again. She promised herself that she wouldn't take no for an answer this time. She was talking to the Radiants about what might be going on with him. Deep in her gut, she felt that it was not some natural occurrence, a reaction to stress from losing his twin brother. It was something more, something evil.

She had checked on the babies before venturing out into the dark hallway that led to bedroom after bedroom. The Radiants had gotten over their fears of being inside and were sleeping in rooms with their daughters, and Penelope and Nancy both had rooms as well. Everyone else had gone back home, leaving some rooms empty once again.

"Amanda." She heard the whisper again and felt a draft pick up and lead her toward the room where all the diaries were kept. Her aunt's diaries fluttered in the invisible wind, and Amanda jumped with fright. The curtains were flying in the air, and she was sure she could see the shape of a woman passing them, running into them to show a piece of her silhouette. Were there such things as ghosts? After learning about werewolves, witches, and fairies, it didn't seem impossible.

However, this was the idea she feared the most; the dead haunting the Earth and messing with the living. A chill ran up her spine, and she wanted to run.

Then, she saw the face, clear as day, definitely a woman with long flowing hair. Her face seemed almost familiar, but she wasn't sure where she'd seen it before. But as it approached, she closed her eyes and put her hands up as if that would protect her. She felt chilled to the bone and then a nausea she couldn't describe as the voice rang through her ears and then finally passed. She looked behind her to see the woman floating away as if she had just passed straight through Amanda's body.

She wasn't wasting anytime; she had to know what was going on. She ran after the ghost woman and saw her stop in front of one of the bedrooms and walk inside. Then, the woman was gone. Amanda wasn't sure which woman had chosen that room, but she did know which room she'd find Catrona in. She ran to the right and knocked on her door, frantically, not caring who else she disturbed. She knew she had probably turned as white as the ghost herself.

Bri, Catrona's daughter, answered the door, rubbing sleep from her eyes.

"I'm so sorry to wake the two of you up, but I think I just saw a ghost."

The door opened further to reveal Catrona in a long red gown. "Well, you certainly look like it; come in."

Amanda followed the women into their room; one of the yellow rooms. The window was open, so the wind was making it a little chilly inside, but she supposed that was the way Catrona liked it.

Bri lay back down on the bed while Catrona sat on the trunk at the end of the bed next to Amanda.

"So, what makes you think you have seen a ghost? Tell me about what's going on," Catrona ordered with a worried look on her face.

"Well, first, before I forget, I want to ask you about my husband, too. Who knows, maybe it's all related." Catrona nodded her on, so she continued, "Over the past week, he's been having nightmares that make him sweat and become restless. One night he was like thrashing and seizing. I had to use my magic to calm him down. He is always startled and looking around when he wakes but can't remember the dream. At first, we thought it was just a side effect of stress and grief over his brother, but now I believe it might be something else. Is that possible?"

Catrona looked thoughtful as she went over what Amanda told her in her head. "Well, there are a few possibilities here, but it's hard to tell without knowing what the dream was. Your first conclusion could be correct, it could be some dark magic messing with him, or his body could even be picking up on this ghost you believe to have seen. I don't know much about werewolves, but perhaps they are sensitive to the supernatural."

"So, ghosts are real; I did see one?" Amanda asked, both afraid and curious.

"It's hard to tell, but it is possible. I have heard that Earth Radiants can see ghosts if their powers are strong enough and honed well enough. Your mother was very powerful, and you have her powers, plus the blood of a werewolf, an alpha werewolf at that. On top of that, you were trained by Ariella, a fairy queen. There's no telling how strong you might become. Your powers could be limitless, which is why your brother wanted them so badly. It's in part why we have agreed to stay, no matter the dangers. Tell me more about the encounter."

Amanda took a deep breath, feeling overwhelmed. Her powers could be limitless? That was actually a scary thought. Could she lose control of them or hurt someone with them?

"A couple of times I've felt this chill and heard whispers of my name when no one was there. It happened again tonight, so I got up to look around in the hall and heard my name again. I followed the voice into the room where my family's journals are kept, and my aunt's journals began to blow open with this huge, cold draft. The curtains were blowing, and I could make out the shape of a woman in them, and then she came toward me, and I saw her face. It looked familiar, but I'm not sure why. Then, she said my name again and came at me. I closed my eyes and felt her walk through me and turned around and followed her out. She walked into one of the rooms and disappeared."

"So, this ghost was a woman and looked familiar. Didn't your aunt live here just before you came?"

Amanda sat up straight as what Catrona was getting at dawned on her. The ghost had rattled her aunt's journals. The face had been familiar because it was similar to her own. "Are you saying it's my aunt? The ghost is my aunt. I can't believe it! All this time I've wished to meet her, and she's been right here. So, how do I communicate with her? What might she want?"

"Well, generally, ghosts don't just hang around for no reason. She probably has a specific task or message she needs or wants to complete. My guess is it has something to do with protecting you or making sure you're safe or something. I'm not sure. I've never seen one. So, this is all speculation. You need to pay attention to everything she does. It could all be clues leading to whatever it is she needs you to know or do. But know that once her task is completed, there won't be some kind of family reunion. She'll move on."

Amanda looked down at the ground as her heart began to ache. It was like a tease, dangling family in front of her that she couldn't even truly talk to or keep. "Okay, well thank you for telling me what you can. I won't keep you any longer." She got up to leave.

"One more thing, Amanda," Catrona said, stopping her in her tracks. "Be very careful. She may very well be your aunt and here to protect you, but there are evil spirits that can take on anyone's likeness to get to you. Don't do anything that feels wrong to you, and don't touch her or anger her if you can help it, until you know for sure if she means you harm or good will. Use your powers when necessary."

Amanda felt a chill run down her spine at the warning, but her heart told her that her aunt was here to help her, that there was something she needed to tell her. She was determined to find out what it was, even if she had to stay up all night to accomplish it.

Amanda thanked Catrona for her help and headed back to her bedroom to check on Romeo. Before she went on a ghost hunt, she wanted to be sure that he was safe and calm. Sure enough, she found him lying there, breathing heavily and drenched in sweat, but the thrashing had stopped. Luckily, he hadn't woken up either of the babies. She smiled down at the three of them and whispered that she loved them before she went back into the hall and closed her eyes, focusing on her aunt. She thought about everything she'd learned from the journals; her love, her strength, and channeled it into calling the ghost to her.

She felt a cold chill come over the hall and herself, and as she opened her eyes, it was cold enough she could see her breath. Then, she heard her name being called very close by. Her eyes followed it to the right and caught a shimmer out of the corner of her eye. Then, the woman appeared, clearer than ever. She almost looked like a live human, taking on a form that looked so similar to her own. The woman was still a little wispy and translucent.

"Amanda…" Her name trailed from the woman's pale pink lips. The woman was so beautiful; she couldn't believe she came from such a family. "Follow me."

Amanda did as her aunt said, following her into the room filled with journals again. This time a journal that looked almost as old as the first one she read from her ancestor rustled back in the far corner. It sprayed dust everywhere as the woman forced it to turn to a page.

"Rose." Her aunt spoke a name that Amanda didn't recognize. But as she picked up the journal, she saw that the name Rose was written just inside the cover. She began to read.

April 7, 1928

My twenty-fourth birthday is not too far off, and I feel like I am the only one my age in town who is not wed. I enjoyed my childhood as my parents allowed, but I am afraid that I am running out of time to find someone. My father has just begun courting a woman named Lil, who has a nephew she wants me to meet. If my father marries this woman, it might be strange to marry her nephew, but I am running out of options. I have agreed to meet him.

Amanda skipped a few entries to see what might be important about this Rose person.

May 17, 1928

I just found out a life-shattering thing tonight, and I am not sure what to do with it. I know that I have to tell Simon what I am, especially since the full moon will be in just one week, but I am afraid our engagement will end abruptly if he knew that I was this monster. My family tells me that I should be proud to come from such a family, especially since my little brother will grow up to be the alpha someday, but all I can think of is being different and a thing of nightmares. How could Simon ever accept me as his wife now that I will turn into a beast each full moon and run around in a fur-covered body?

May 20, 1928

I told Simon today, and it went better than I thought, or sort of did. I found out something disturbing about Simon as well. He is a witch and so is his aunt. He can do magic, which means that any children we have will be able to as well. But I know my family will disapprove, and I am not so keen on the idea either. People don't think highly of witchcraft here, and being associated with it could be dangerous. When I voiced my concerns, his aunt walked in and asked to talk to me privately. She threatened me with dark magic, saying all the things she could do to me or my family if I didn't make her nephew happy. I am so afraid. I would take being an old maid any day over all of this.

Until my next thoughts, I bid adieu.

The entries stopped after that, and Amanda could feel the hair standing up on the back of her neck. So, witches had plagued her family from the beginning it seemed, but why? And the fact that the girl, Rose, called her betrothed's mother Lil made her suspect that her real name was Lilith. Everything seemed to lead back to Lilith or Elena, or whoever she was. Then, Amanda remembered something, the story that Romeo had told her about how werewolves came to be. Wasn't the woman's name Lilith? Could it be a coincidence?

She didn't think so. Nothing in her life lately was ever that simple.

Amanda's head shot up, and she looked at her aunt, who was surveying her. She looked even more real, and Amanda wondered if she could talk. "You are my aunt, aren't you?"

The woman nodded with what appeared to be a kind smile on her face.

Amanda let one tear run down her face at the knowledge that in some way she did get to meet this incredible woman. "I wish I could get to know you, to love you."

"No time," the woman whispered, reaching out to Amanda.

"Is the Lilith from the story about Fenris the same as the Lilith who was in league with Dean and his uncle?"

Her aunt nodded, sadly.

Amanda felt her heart skip a beat. "Why? What does she want?"

"Power, always power," her aunt responded. "She infected Fenris; she created the gene. She was the first dark witch and was cast out for it. So, this was how she would get power, by birthing a race that could defeat the Radiants, overpower them. Fenris killed himself when he found out and took it to the grave. The alpha line passed to her son, and he suspected her of something and cut her out. Ever since she has tried to worm her way back in."

Amanda couldn't believe that her aunt was walking and talking right in front of her. It was amazing and scary all at once.

"But beware, my precious niece. You have the power she needs to get back in. You are married to the alpha, and you are a Radiant. She will stop at nothing, including disguising herself to trick you and those you love."

Her aunt's words rang through her head like a bell. Nancy; she was talking about Nancy, wasn't she? How had Amanda been so blind as to trust a stranger just because she seemed to know things? It was ridiculous. She was about to thank her aunt and ask her what to do when she heard growls, bangs, and screams coming from everywhere in the house it seemed.

Amanda rushed out into the hall to see what was going on. If her babies or Romeo had been harmed, she'd never forgive herself. She ran to her bedroom to check on her children and Romeo to find that Romeo was not there. She cast a quick protection spell over the door to protect Jason and Sarina before searching for him. Instead, she found Catrona's door wide open.

Amanda made her way inside, being vigilant about every sound and every dark corner. Lilith could be hiding anywhere. But as she entered the room, she saw Bri crouched over her mother, tears coming from her eyes. Suddenly, Bri stood up and was consumed by flames, fire rising into the air all around her. Amanda could feel the heat, and stifled a scream as they died down just as suddenly to reveal Bri safe and sound.

"What's going on?" Amanda's eyes darted between Bri and Catrona on the floor, knowing deep down what had just occurred but so unwilling to accept it.

"She gave me her power, right before….right before…" Bri blubbered, seemingly unable to form a complete thought in her grief.

"No!" Amanda screamed, falling onto the floor at Catrona's side. There was no way that Lilith could have killed Catrona, the leader of the Radiants. She was the most experienced, the most powerful of them all. How could Lilith trick her and kill her? No one had that much power, or did they?

"There's nothing we can do, no magic to save her. She knew it was coming, Amanda. That's why we came here. I just didn't know it would be like this. We need to find the others. They could be in danger, too." Bri was still in tears but had become the voice of reason. She was so much like Catrona, Amanda knew Bri was the right person to take her place, if anyone could.

"You're right," Amanda sighed, giving Catrona a kiss on the forehead before picking herself up. They could lose more lives tonight if they didn't find the other Radiants.

They found Penelope and Elijah in the hallway, holding each other as Penelope screamed and cried, almost inconsolable. Amanda didn't want to disturb them, knowing how they felt for each other and that he was the best equipped to calm her, but she had to know everything was okay.

"Penelope, are you all right?" As she asked, Bri nodded down the hall to signal she was going to check on the others. Amanda nodded in agreement and turned her attention back to Penelope.

Elijah spoke for her. "I caught that Nancy woman trying to kill Penelope. I couldn't sleep and was walking around, and I heard screams and came running. Penelope was begging for her life and wanting to know why her friend was doing this to her, but Nancy was crazed and didn't look like herself at all. Then, she ran off when I threatened to turn into a wolf. Is anyone else hurt?"

Amanda got down on the floor with them and rubbed Penelope's back as Elijah held her tight to keep her from totally losing it. What must Penelope think, knowing that a friend tried to kill her? Amanda nodded at Elijah to answer his question without upsetting Penelope further. Her friend wasn't ready to hear that they'd lost their leader yet.

Elijah's eyes got wide with fear for his family and friends, but luckily said nothing out loud yet and turned his attentions back to Penelope as more people joined them in the hall. Alessandra and her daughter, as well as Bri and Aurora, came rushing out to see what had happened.

"What do you need us to do?" Alessandra asked with sad eyes.

Amanda stood up, ready to take charge of the situation. There would be time to grieve and explain later, but Romeo was missing, and her own life and the lives of her children were at stake. "Aurora, please watch my children, keep them safe. I need to find my husband. When I went to check, he was out of bed, and I can't find him anywhere. He's been having nightmares, strange ones, and I have no doubt now that dark magic has played a part. Meet back at the house in one hour so that we can regroup and see what's going on. I'll explain everything then."

Amanda took off running down the stairs and saw the form of her aunt begin to appear, leading her toward Romeo, she was sure. She trusted the ghost implicitly as she led Amanda outside. In the distance, toward the mountains, she could see Romeo moving slowly forward. He seemed in a trance and moved unnaturally. He was too far away for her to catch up with, so she did the only thing she could think; closed her eyes and felt her powers. She caused an earthquake, sure that the town would just think it was normal by now. Romeo's body shook and fell to the ground. She used the earth to propel her forward with each quake until she reached him.

"Romeo, Romeo!" She shook him awake and let out the breath she'd been holding as he opened his eyes and looked around. She folded her body over him in a joyous embrace and helped him up from the ground.

"What happened?" he asked, as the sun began to rise over the snow-capped mountains.

"I think we need to talk about those nightmares of yours. Let's go inside and find everyone else. You missed a lot while you were asleep."

Romeo gave her a worried look, but followed her back into the house as she thought about what the next move might be.

Chapter Five

Elijah scooped up Penelope in his arms and carried her back into her room to lay her down on her bed. Her tears had dried, though her face was still swollen and red from crying and screaming. He wanted to tell her how beautiful she was and how glad he was he'd saved her in time, but he knew there was no point. She would never stand up to the other Radiants, never quit being one to be with him. It wasn't like he thought he was worth all that trouble, but it hurt him so to know where her loyalties were, that he was second in her heart always, when she was first in his.

He left her on the bed and went to walk out of the room before he heard her soft, sniffling voice calling to him. "Elijah?"

He turned around, his heart swelling against his will, and tried to look neutral as he walked back over to her side. "Yes, Penelope?"

"It's okay if you say no, but would you stay with me for a moment? I don't know if I can be alone right now. It's just so much."

His demeanor softened at her request. Part of him knew it was wrong to lie with her, knowing how he felt. It would hurt when he finally had to leave her.

Elijah walked the rest of the way over and got into the bed, trying not to touch her as he did. But she made it impossible, scooting over to him and laying her head on his chest. He tried to keep his hands behind his head so he didn't reciprocate, but as he felt her body quake again with silent tears, he couldn't do it anymore. He stroked her hair. An indescribable ache hurt him so bad he couldn't stand it. The only relief was to have her as his own, and that was never going to happen.

He continued to stroke her hair, and she looked up at him, some of the blond tendrils stuck to the tears on her face. He wiped each one away.

"Is something wrong?" she whispered, and it sounded like music. He had to show her, had to tell her what she was to him, even if it got him nowhere. He knew that it didn't matter who he met, they would never come close to her; he would always love her.

He dared to lean down and kiss her like he'd never kissed anyone. He felt passion as their tongues slipped together, even as more tears rolled down her face. He wasn't sure if she was crying about the loss of her friend, almost being killed, or because she could feel the same pain he did. As he pulled away, the words spilled from his mouth before he could stop them. "I love you."

Her face changed to shock, and her hand flew up to cover her mouth. Obviously, she had not been expecting those words, had not known how he felt. "Say something," he begged, not realizing until that moment how bad it felt to say that to someone and not have them say it back. He found himself wishing and hoping that she would say it back.

"I don't know what to say, Elijah. I'm afraid; I'm so afraid. Being a Radiant is all I have, and I want to say I'd give up myself, no matter what, to be with you, to say those words back to you like I want to. But I don't know how to let go. I'm not Amanda. I'm not strong and bold and sure of everything."

"So, you're telling me that you feel the same way but you won't say it? I'm not asking for you to give anything up for me, to run away with me into the sunset or something. But I have to know if you feel that way, too." Elijah found himself feeling desperate as his breathing came in gasps. He was panicking and had no idea what to do with himself.

"If I say it, I'll have to do those things. I don't think I can strip myself down emotionally for you and then not get to have you."

"Then, have me," he ordered, crushing his lips over hers again. Her heart beat fast and hard in her chest, her whole body was responding to his touch. But she suddenly stiffened and pulled away.

"I think it's been an hour," she said. "We better get downstairs."

Amanda looked around her at all the people she loved and realized at that moment what was on the line. Aurora had called Audri and her father, so even they were there as well as Benjamin. It was a bitter sweet moment, seeing relationships healing and possibly coming together while the leader of the Radiants lay dead upstairs. Romeo had helped her get Catrona into the bed until they could figure out what else to do. The woman remained beautiful and made Amanda think about Snow White asleep encased in glass.

"I know all of you are wondering what has happened overnight. I've gathered you all because we are in danger, and we have to work together to make sure we are all kept safe." She glanced down at the child in her arms and then the little boy to her right being held by Audri. She had to protect them at any cost. "The woman who was staying with us was not Nancy Santos. Unfortunately, this means that the real Nancy Santos is most likely deceased, since powerful dark magic can allow a witch to absorb appearances as well as powers of those they kill. The woman who called herself Nancy was actually Lilith."

Gasps went around the room, and Romeo squeezed her leg. She had yet to fully explain it to him, and she knew how much it would hurt. She remembered how he had told her that Elena was different at first and later became a problem. What if Lilith had killed her after she met Damon and took her identity? How bad would that make Romeo feel about the whole thing?

"Lilith is also more than you think. She can assume the identity of many people and poses a great danger to all of us. She is not the silly accomplice we thought she was; she is actually a very old and powerful witch. She is the very Lilith who wed Fenris and birthed him his first child."

"No, that's not possible. That was centuries ago, and the Lilith from the story was not a witch!" Aurora cried.

Amanda looked at her sympathetically. Their worlds were all turning upside down, and she understood how they must feel about it. Her life had just done the same not too long ago.

"Apparently it's not impossible. She was the first dark witch, and when she was scorned for using dark magic, she went off on her own to find a way to be the one in power. Birthing a family of werewolves with magic was how she thought she'd do it. Her family found out and cut her out of their lives, so she's plagued the werewolves ever since, trying to get involved in the most powerful families to try again. That's why she wanted Romeo and what she wants with me. She's been doing this for centuries. She absorbs power to stay alive. So, she has the powers of thousands of witches, and she's after us."

Amanda stopped and looked around to see faces filled with fear and shock. No one seemed to know what to say. She didn't really know what to say either. There was no comfort to give.

Before Amanda could do anything, the door burst open and wind and rain swirled through the house. A woman entered the family room, looking like a she-devil. Her eyes were red and so was her hair, which was blown back and dripping wet. She wore a crimson cape over a black dress. If she wasn't so evil, and her teeth didn't resemble fangs, the woman might be beautiful. Amanda was sure of who it was. There was no doubt in her mind that Lilith stood in her house in her true form. She wanted to pick up her children and run forever, but she knew that would accomplish nothing. She had to beat Lilith at her own game. It was the only way.

"I'm so sorry to interrupt your little pow wow," Lilith hissed out, sounding more like a reptile than a human being, "but I have some unfinished business with a few of you. But first, I think I should introduce myself. My name is Lilith." She gave a mocking bow as she began to cackle, the unearthly sound echoing through the whole house over the sound of the howling wind.

Amanda knew she would have to be quick if she was going to catch her off guard and save them all.

Amanda passed Sarina to Romeo and stood up in one move, ready to use the storm against Lilith, but Lilith saw it coming. In one swoop of her hand, she had Romeo, along with both children. Amanda felt like she was being wrapped up in barbed wire and choked as the evil woman ran her fingers along each of their faces. She had taken what was most precious to Amanda, and there was nothing she could do now or Lilith would kill them. She was sure of it. She could never save them all.

"I know that look, Amanda, I've seen it many times before. You know you've lost. No matter how powerful you are, you aren't powerful enough. The only one of you who might have stopped me is dead. So, are you ready to make a deal with me?"

Amanda wanted to hide, wanted to run, but she was stuck, immovable. There was no other choice. She couldn't let anyone else get involved, when it was her family on the line. She held her palm back to still everyone who dared to move against Lilith, afraid that there would be no escape for her children if someone made a move. "What is it you want with me, Lilith?"

Lilith let out her terrible cackle again, and Amanda wanted to gag. Tears started to fill her eyes as the loves of her life were encircled in the evil woman's arms. She'd never seen Romeo look quite so helpless.

"You know what's sad about this whole thing? If things were different, we could've been friends. Amanda. You and I are so alike in many ways, headstrong, powerful…. But it doesn't matter, does it? Because I want from you what everyone else wants; to be you, to have what you have."

Amanda closed her eyes and took a deep breath, trying to calm herself. "Of course," she said, opening her eyes again. "You want me to give you my power, just like Dean did. If you just let them go, you can have it, all of it. I just want my family."

"Oh dear, Amanda, I thought you were smarter than that."

Amanda narrowed her eyes at Lilith's words, fearful as to what she could mean.

"I don't just want your power; I want to be you. You are part werewolf and part Radiant; one of a kind. You are married to the alpha in a powerful line of werewolves and have mated with him to create two beautiful and incredibly powerful children. All this, and you didn't even know who or what you were just over a year ago. It's such a waste. I want it, and I deserve it. But I'm willing to compromise. I want your husband. All you have to do is let me take him with me, and I will give you back your children and promise that no harm will ever come to them by my hand whilst they are still under age."

Amanda held back a sob and wondered what made Lilith think that was a good enough deal. She would lose Romeo and eventually could lose her children anyway as soon as they came of age. It was too much to bear. She was ready to lose herself, knowing that she'd never live through that kind of pain.

"What good would it do you to have Romeo? We are mated. He can't feel anything for you, no matter what you do." Amanda tried to sound confident, but she knew it was useless. If Lilith created everything having to do with werewolves, she could probably undo it as well, including the bond.

"Firstly, as you can see, I'm not beyond using threats to get what I want. I can threaten you and your children and all his family forever, if that's what it takes to get what I want, which is a bloodline linked to me that becomes powerful, much like you, Amanda. Secondly, my power is enough to make him want me in those moments. I can't override your bond, but I can make him forget for an hour or two on occasion, and that's all I need. Because once I have his children, he's not going to abandon them. He's not like that. He's a noble man. And then, when the time is right, those children will help me take down the Radiants and make the whole world bow to me. Then, everyone will know how powerful I am and what I deserve."

Amanda was horrified at her words. She looked at Romeo for help, for a sign that he wasn't going to allow this to happen. She could see that he was looking back at her and holding back tears. She felt like she was going to collapse right there.

Then, she felt someone clasp her hand on each side, and Bri pushed forward in front of them. Amanda tried to pull her back, but her determination made her impossible to stop. She could feel Penelope and Alessandra begin to link all of them together, waiting for Bri to grab on. Bri approached Lilith, and Lilith looked on, both amused and curious. Lilith obviously didn't think Bri was capable of much or she would have already made a move.

Suddenly, Bri reached out her hand, and Lilith burst into flames and began screeching unnaturally. Amanda screamed for her to stop it or she'd burn her family up, too. Bri latched onto the rest of Radiants to complete the linking as the flames died down, revealing a blackened Lilith with tattered and burnt clothes. She had let go of Jason, and Romeo caught him on his back, having been able to change in all the chaos. At least they were safe, but Lilith reached to grab them all once again.

"Now!" Bri called as they were linked, and the power surged through them. They came at Lilith in a line, chanting various spells, pulling the darkness out of her along with all the souls she'd taken in her thousands of years. As she writhed on the ground, Romeo pulled away, leaving a chunk of hair in her hand as he went to stand with his family behind them. Amanda gave him a fleeting look as they descended on the woman who had collapsed, speaking telepathically to let them know to get to safety. She could feel their power even stronger than she ever had, and she knew the toll it would take on the land.

They pushed her out the door, and she was swirling around in the wind as shadows and pieces ripped from her body. All her power was leaving her, one death at a time. Amanda looked in the distance to see black clouds full of lightning rolling in. Tornadoes began to spring to life everywhere, tearing up the land as they continued to focus on Lilith. It was exhausting them, bringing her down to a level they could deal with. She was swollen with the power of so many witches. It was sad to think how many people had died at her hands.

Then, the moment came, as the earth cracked and trees toppled to the ground, one crushing Lilith's weak body. As Amanda looked down on her, she could see how gaunt and pale she was, no longer a beautiful she-devil but just an old decrepit zombie. Her hair had lost almost all color, and she was begging for her life, for mercy. But the Radiants had made their decision. She was to be executed for her crimes and the earth would be free of her evil forever.

Alessandra called on the rain to pour over Lilith and drown her in its tumultuous waves as Penelope took the breath from her lungs. Lilith wilted before them as the water subsided, and Amanda reached down to pull the heart from her body and held it out to Bri. Bri stared it down until it burst into flames, turning into ash. No one would be able to take her power or revive her. Her heart was gone in the wind as her body melted into the earth.

Amanda turned her head away, back toward the house. She couldn't look at the devastation before her. The storm was still going on, though slightly calmer than before, and she could barely make out Romeo standing near the back door. She ran to him, the wind fighting against her every step of the way, and collapsed to the ground in his arms with tears streaming from her eyes. Her body could no longer contain her emotions as they came at her all at once. She had been directly responsible for so much death and destruction that she didn't think she'd recognize herself in a mirror anymore.

"It's over, Amanda; it's finally over," Romeo soothed her in her ear while stroking her back. She could hear her children wailing from within the house now, afraid of the storm and most likely hungry. But she knew someone else would be happy to take care of them, because she could not move from that spot without falling apart. She needed her husband to hold her together.

"It's all over, and everyone's safe now. She's gone, Amanda. Please, look at me."

Amanda dared to pull away enough to see him smiling at her, and he began kissing every inch of her face and neck in desperation. He was overwhelming her with love so that she couldn't feel the pain.

"You're okay," she squeaked out, realizing it for the first time. "You're here and alive and still in love with me. I was so afraid that… Oh, Romeo." She collapsed onto him, knocking him completely flat on the ground. A mixture of tears and laughter filled the air as the sky continued to pelt them with hail and water. The Radiants and their family passed them into the house, and they stayed there holding each other.

"Of course, I'm here. You don't ever have to be afraid that you'll lose me for any reason. No magic is strong enough to take me away from you," Romeo said with conviction before standing up with her in his arms, carrying her over the threshold like it was their wedding night all over again. They dripped all over the beautiful wood floors.

"Penelope, a little help!" Amanda called with an exasperated laugh. Penelope appeared in front of them, cradling Sarina in her arms with a bottle in the baby's mouth. Penelope gave a sweet smile and puckered her lips, causing a wind to surround the both of them like a giant blow dryer, and they became instantly dry.

They headed into the family room, hand in hand, to a round of applause from the whole family. Amanda began hugging everyone, finally appreciating the family she had acquired. She was so glad they were all safe and sound. It made her think of her aunt and wonder what had become of the ghost who had tried to warn her of the evil within her own home. When no one was looking, she snuck away upstairs to look around, hoping to catch one more glimpse of the woman she was so often compared to. The woman who had her money and a home.

She found her in the room she used to sleep in herself, trying with no avail to smooth over the comforter. "Is it really you?" Amanda whispered, not wanting to scare her away. The woman looked more see-through than before, like she was fading away.

"Yes, Amanda, it is me, your aunt. But I must go soon. My work is done here. The love of my life has moved on in his life, and I have protected you the way I always meant to."

Amanda sat down on the bed next to her aunt, and her aunt placed a hand on Amanda's knee. Even though Amanda couldn't feel the weight on her, it was a gesture she'd needed. She'd been waiting so long to feel the love of family again, and she didn't want the moment to end.

"Thank you for everything. I wish we could have known each other," Amanda sniffled.

"I know," the woman said with kind eyes before looking toward the door. Amanda followed her eyes to see that Romeo had come in to see what she was doing. "Go on, you two take care of each other. He is the perfect match for you, always has been. He's loved you from day one. I can promise that."

Amanda started crying again, knowing the words were true. Why she'd ever tried to resist the amazing man who had become her husband and the father to her children, she wasn't sure.

"What's going on?" Romeo asked, coming to her side. Of course, he could not see her aunt sitting on the other side of her.

Amanda looked back at her aunt to see her nodding and smiling, her form fading into blackness. It was time for her to move on to wherever she was meant to be; beyond life and earth. "Just thinking about some things and saying goodbye." She leaned in and kissed him hard on the lips.

He gave a slight chuckle. "What was that for?"

"Just because I love you, Romeo, more than I ever could have imagined possible."

"I love you, too, and those beautiful children you gave me. Speaking of…"

They stood up, holding hands, to head back down the stairs and heard a chorus of cheering and whistles coming from the family room. They took the stairs down two at a time and almost ran into a clapping and smiling Elijah.

"What's going on?" Romeo asked him.

"Benjamin finally asked Audri to marry him. They want to get married as soon as possible."

"Oh my gosh!" Amanda squealed. "It looks like everyone is finally coming together like they should." She instantly regretted what she said when Elijah looked sad and walked off. She had almost forgotten about him and Penelope and how they'd held each other. If only there was something she could do for them.

Amanda felt a tap on her shoulder and turned around to find Alessandra and her daughter standing behind her. "I don't mean to interrupt a happy moment, but we have some work to do. The earth needs some repairing, and then we will have to part. The land cannot take any more of our powers together."

Amanda walked out the door with the other Radiants, her head hung in somber silence. They really had done quite of bit of damage, and she almost felt hopeless about it. Was there really a way to repair everything?

"How do we fix this?" Amanda asked, surveying the soaked and split earth all around her. She could almost feel the pain pulsing from the ground.

"You just have to believe," Penelope whispered, squeezing her hand. Amanda knew what she meant and remembered her powers might be limitless as their friend Catrona had said. It was up to her, the Earth Radiant, to believe in herself and her powers to heal the land. So, that's exactly what she did.

Chapter Six

Amanda looked out toward the mountains, past the crowd that had gathered for Benjamin and Audri's reception. It had been a long day of festivities. The Radiants had all gathered in the mountains that morning to lay Catrona to rest after they had finally finished repairing the land. Then, it had been time to decorate for the wedding of the century. Audri had specifically asked to get married on Amanda's estate, and of course she'd said yes.

It had been a beautiful and short ceremony leading into a huge party. She'd never seen Audri look so elegant and shining with happiness. Maybe Aurora wasn't going to be the bubbly one anymore.

Once the reception was over, the Radiants were supposed to meet one more time to crown Bri and say goodbye. It was something Amanda was dreading. There were still occasional earthquakes because of their power, so she knew it was necessary. But the thought of being alone scared her. She had Romeo and her children, but no other witches. She wasn't even sure Penelope was going to stay, since it would be so painful being around Elijah. What was she going to do without her new best friend by her side?

Looking to her right, she could see that Penelope was sipping on some champagne and chatting with Elijah, probably discussing her plans to leave. It was so bitter sweet watching everyone else get happy endings while Penelope and Elijah would suffer forever. Love, as far as Amanda knew, didn't really go away with time. They would always think about each other. But she supposed not everyone could get what they wanted, and she couldn't exactly say that she'd trade places with her.

Amanda went back inside where more people talked around the dining room table with drinks in their hand. Apparently, many werewolves had been invited to the wedding as a sort of political move. Romeo wanted to make sure there was peace for a very long time, and she couldn't help but agree. She made her way upstairs and into her bedroom where she kissed the tops of Jason's and Sarina's heads. They were both in matching cribs now, and Romeo had made them fit in the room with them. Amanda couldn't stand to sleep without them near her.

"Amanda," Bri called from the hallway.

Amanda came out of the room and shut the door as softly as possible.

"It's time, Amanda," Bri said.

Amanda nodded and followed Bri out front, where the others were already waiting.

"Are we ready to begin?" Bri asked, grasping Alessandra's hand, but Alessandra pulled away.

Everyone looked at her with questions in their eyes, and Alessandra looked around at each one of them.

"I have made a decision, after much thinking. Lucia, can you please step forward?" Lucia, looking quite shocked and confused took her mother's hand and came to the center of the other women. "My dear friend, Catrona, has passed on, leaving her powers to her daughter, Bri. All three of you are very young, and I know that my time is coming as well. I believe it is time for a new generation of Radiants. I would like to try passing on my powers to Lucia before the ceremony, if you all agree to that."

Amanda wasn't sure what to say. Lucia had always come off as shy and quiet, and she couldn't imagine being the leaders of the witches without Alessandra or Catrona. But ultimately, it was going to happen one way or the other. Everyone else seemed speechless, too.

Finally Bri spoke, clearing her throat awkwardly. "Whatever you believe is best should be done."

With that, Alessandra closed her eyes and so did Lucia, clinging to each other's hands. They began to light up, blinding all of the Radiants, until finally, Alessandra collapsed to the ground. A small scream escaped Lucia's throat before both were dull and on their feet again.

"It is done," Lucia said in a squeaky voice. She came forward and joined hands as they all formed a circle like they had done once before with the older women. Amanda could feel the new power pulsating through them, going from one to another. This group of

Radiants felt different, even more powerful. Could that even be possible?

"Do you feel that?" Penelope asked, looking over at Amanda.

"I do," everyone else said at once. It was intoxicating.

"All right, are you ready to become our queen, Bri?" Lucia asked with a friendly smile.

Bri shook her head. "I've been thinking about something, and it's going to sound like a crazy idea. But I do not know that I have the right to lead. I am so young and have just barely begun my training. I know that the two of you may feel the same." She nodded to Penelope and Amanda. "But I feel the two of you are more equipped to be our leaders. Penelope, you actually have the most experience of the four of us, and Amanda, your powers are limitless. I want us to vote on who should be the leader, just to be fair. I think it may be time for things to be different."

Lucia nodded in approval along, with her mother in the background. She started off the voting. "The leader has always been the most powerful, so I think it should be Amanda," she answered matter-of-factly.

Amanda felt her eyes go wide. She wasn't quite sure she was prepared for this twist.

"I second that decision," Penelope spoke up, loudly.

Amanda elbowed her in the ribs and looked at her. Penelope just smiled and nodded to Bri, who also agreed. That meant that Amanda was their leader, period.

"The job is yours if you will accept it, Amanda," Bri said.

Amanda found herself nodding, knowing in her heart that even though she was afraid, it was the right decision. "All right, the decision is made. Let us begin the ceremony."

They pushed Amanda forward as they formed a line in front of her. She felt like she was having an out-of-body experience, looking at the three women who were about to make her their queen. She was the queen of her werewolf pack, a Radiant witch, and soon to be the queen of all witches. What an amazing life this was.

"We gather here today as Radiants numbering four, to crown a new leader. We have voted in good faith and chosen Amanda, the current Earth Radiant, to be our reigning queen until she can no longer perform that duty and wishes to pass her powers onto the next generation." Bri spoke with an authority much like her mother's, and it began to fill the hole Catrona had left in all of their hearts. "Lucia, if you would start the blessings."

Lucia stepped forward with her bouncy hair and shining eyes and curtsied in front of Amanda. "I, Lucia, the Water Radiant, pledge my fealty to Amanda, the Earth Radiant, as our new reigning queen. I bless her and her family with the gift of happy tears. May the water that flows from your eyes not always be in sadness, but also in the joy of everyday life."

Amanda blinked, unsure of what to think of all of it. She was so new to everything, and it was all happening so fast. But she needed to slow it down and capture the moment in her brain. It was going to be a part of her forever.

Penelope stepped forward next, bowing with a smile and a giggle. Her blond hair shone in the moonlight and made her resemble a ghost, and Amanda smiled back at her friend. "I Penelope, the Wind Radiant, pledge myself to Amanda, the Earth Radiant, as our new reigning queen. You are my best friend and my newfound sister. I think you are getting everything you deserve. What I would like to bless you with is a dual gift of love and belief. We often hear people speak of the wind as a metaphor for things that exist that we cannot see. I wish for the wind to grant you the knowledge that you are never alone. Your family and friends are watching you and believe in you, and you will know this each time a warm breeze caresses your cheek."

Amanda felt a tear stream down her face as the wind came and carried it away. That was the best gift she could think of. Penelope gave her the love of her parents and her aunt and even Catrona.

Penelope stepped back, and Bri took her place. "I, Bri, Fire Radiant, pledge my fealty to Amanda, the Earth Radiant, as our new reigning queen. I bless her with the passion and everlasting vigor of a blazing fire. Just as a flame fights and never dies and burns within each one of us with passion, I bless you with this as our leader. You will always fight for what you believe to be right and prevail, even when the situation seems to be impossible."

Bri stepped back and the three joined hands and bowed low to Amanda, beginning to chant a spell that Amanda recognized. It was the one she memorized for the ceremony that was supposed to involve crowning Bri, not herself. The crown began to weigh heavy on her head, and she stood up straight and proud as the three women looked on her with loyalty as her subjects. It suddenly felt so real and so right, like it was what she was always meant to do.

"So, you are now our leader. Do you have any laws or declarations for us before we part ways?" Bri asked softly. Amanda thought for a moment, wondering what she could do to show her appreciation. Then, her eyes met Penelope's, and she knew exactly what she needed to do. She could finally do what she had wished for so long.

"I do have a ruling I would like to make." Her voice sounded so regal, she didn't even recognize it. "I rule that from this day forward any Radiant or witch has the right to love and marry anyone who is deemed a suitable match for him or her, even if they are of human or other supernatural decent."

As she finished, Penelope leapt into the air with a victorious scream. She went to each of the Radiants and said a quick goodbye with a hug and a kiss before approaching Amanda. "You have no idea what this means to me. I can never thank you enough."

Amanda pulled her into a tight embrace with a small chuckle. "Go to him, Penelope. You can thank me later!" she ordered, laughing as Penelope ran around to the back where the reception was breaking up. She knew that they were going to have a lot to talk about in the morning, if the two of them were done by then.

Then, she looked to the remaining two women who stood before her and felt a sadness in her heart, but nothing needed to be said. She could feel what they felt as they turned and walked away. It was time for them to go home. But she had a feeling she wouldn't be alone. Elijah was sure to keep Penelope around for a long time.

"Elijah, can I talk with you for a moment?" Penelope asked timidly, tapping him on the shoulder. She had been so excited on the way over, and now she found herself shaky and nervous. She felt some embarrassment at the fact that she hadn't stood up for her feelings before without that law being in place. She wouldn't blame him if he didn't even want her anymore because she hadn't defied who she was for his love. But she had to try. Her heart ached so badly, especially after that kiss they had shared after her near-death experience with Lilith.

Elijah turned and looked around him as if he was making sure no one else had asked for him. Penelope felt about five inches tall.

"Okay," he finally said, following her into the house. Many of the guests had already gone home.

Only a few friends and family members remained. Penelope led him into a room that had been converted into an office and slid the doors closed. She knew that Romeo and Amanda were upstairs and didn't want to disturb them.

"What is this all about?" Elijah sounded both curious and amused, and she wasn't sure how to begin. Part of her wanted to fly into his arms and begin kissing him, but the reasonable part of her knew she had to do this the right way.

"I just came from a meeting with the Radiants. We crowned our new queen."

"Oh," Elijah breathed, sitting down on the love seat in the corner. It wasn't going the right way, and she didn't know how to make him understand.

"Amanda is our queen now, and she made a ruling about love and marriage so that now we can marry whoever we want. Isn't that great?"

He nodded, not meeting her eyes. "I'm happy for all of you. You should be able to marry whoever you want. So, who's the lucky guy?" Elijah asked bitterly.

Penelope's heart shattered for him. Had she ruined their relationship forever or misread things? Apparently, she was going to have to make it clear.

She got down in front of him on her knees and tried to get him to meet her eyes. He looked her up and down like she was vermin, but she spoke to him anyway. She couldn't hold it back anymore. "I thought maybe it could be you?" It came out more like a question than a statement. Her confidence was wavering, and she needed him to step up and say something.

"Oh, so now that your queen says it's okay, I'm suddenly good enough for you? Did she order you to marry me?" he burst out in anger and stepped over her, almost stepping on her.

"Please, don't act this way. I know I should have stepped up and said something before. I'm weak and terrible. You're the one who's too good for me. But I love you, and I can't help that. So, please don't be angry with me."

Elijah came at her and lifted her off the floor like she weighed nothing, forcing her to stand up. His brows were wrinkled in anger, and their faces were almost touching.

"What did you just say?" he asked, more softly than she expected.

"Not to be angry with me."

"No, before that," he demanded, shaking her a little.

"Oh, that I love you. And I do, Elijah. I've loved you for so long, and I should have said it sooner."

He placed her onto the couch, letting her fall with a thud as he began to pace back and forth, mumbling under his breath. Penelope suddenly feared he had lost his mind or she had said the wrong thing.

"You love me?" he asked, turning around and looking straight at her. He suddenly looked like an innocent little boy.

She nodded fervently.

"And you want to use the new law to marry me?"

It was such a strange line of questioning, and Penelope felt unsure as to what he was getting at. She nodded anyway. There was no other honest answer to give.

Then, he flew at her, and at first she felt fear, until he gently landed his body over hers, forcing her to lay down. "You have no idea how crazy I've driven myself, waiting to hear those words from your lips." As he spoke, his breath landed on her parted lips. She could smell and taste his musk, and she felt like her body was on fire with him so close like that.

Without another word spoken, he crashed his lips over hers, and their tongues slipped into each other's mouths. His hand crept up her leg to her thigh, and her body screamed for him. She was so scared, never having experienced anything like that, but she let him go on as he lifted her skirt up to reveal her red panties underneath. She let out a sigh into his mouth as his fingers slipped inside of them, stroking at her clit. She had no idea until that moment what she had been missing all that time without him, and she wanted to make up for lost time.

With shaky hands, she began to unbutton his shirt to reveal his tan and muscular chest. She let her finger explore every muscle, and she heard him growl low and soft at her touch. It gave her the confidence she needed, and she helped him remove his belt and slacks, revealing black silk boxers swollen with his stiffness. She couldn't believe she was able to make him feel the way he made her feel.

Cold air hit her as he pulled her panties down and then she watched as his boxers slipped to the ground. She allowed herself a moment to worship at the altar of his beautiful body. He was sculpted like some artist had designed him specifically for women to look at. Her eyes finally landed on his hard shaft, standing at attention for her and she held back a gasp.

Her hands encircled his shaft, and she was surprised at how baby soft the skin was there. He closed his eyes, enjoying the warmth of her skin on his sensitive member. She gave it a few long, slow strokes, listening to the soft moans come from his mouth as she pleasured him with her hand. Then, using the hand on his shaft and another on the back of his neck, she guided his body back down, spreading her legs. She was ready to find out what it felt like to have him inside of her.

"Are you sure?" he asked with sweetness as she felt the head of his cock sitting at her entrance.

She nodded, knowing that it was absolutely what she wanted.

"I love you," he whispered into her ear as he finally entered her, slowly at first and then pulled back just to enter again more quickly.

She felt a sharp pain for just a moment and then it eased as she felt warm inside where he was filling her up.

"I love you, too," she responded between gasps of pleasure as he began to pick up speed. Something in the both of them let go and they began to rock to a fast and hard rhythm, breathing heavily as they kissed each other everywhere they could reach. Then, Penelope felt her legs begin to shake against her will, and she couldn't control them. She clung to Elijah tightly, and he growled.

Then, she felt her center began to squeeze his cock tight inside of her and pulse. She screamed and latched onto his back with her nails, causing him to arch his back.

"Yes!" he called out as he reached his climax as well, releasing his wet warmth inside of her. She kissed him, shutting her eyes tight as her body continued to quake and writhe. She wondered if it would ever calm.

"Please, don't leave me, Penelope. Don't change your mind. I want you to be mine. I want you to marry me," Elijah whispered, still hanging on tight.

Penelope swelled with happiness, and tears came streaming out of her eyes in response. She couldn't believe the moment had finally come when she didn't have to hide her feelings for this glorious man anymore and she could give all of herself to him.

"I won't ever leave. I want to be your wife." She pulled away and relaxed, looking up at him with the most genuine smile she'd ever had across her face. He was still inside of her, and her body screamed for more just looking at his amazing body again.

"Maybe we should move this to a more comfortable location," Elijah suggested with a laugh, and he helped her up the stairs into her room where they stayed for the rest of the night, constantly saying out loud the three words they had both held in for so long.

<<◇>>

Amanda retired to her room, where she found Romeo already waiting for her, looking down at the two sleeping babies with a smile. He was an amazing husband but an even more perfect father.

She snuck up behind him and wrapped her arms around his rock-hard body and squeezed. "So, when do you want to make some more of those?" she whispered, jokingly.

He stood still for a moment, still looking down at their children before suddenly whipping around and forcing her onto the bed. It happened so fast it took all the breath out of her body. "I'll go for another two any time you want, my love," he answered with a growl.

His eyes sparkled as he looked down at her, and her heart swelled with love and her body responded to his closeness. "You make such beautiful children, and the process is so much fun." He began kissing up her neck and tickling her thighs, making her giggle in response.

"I'd have to wholeheartedly agree with that one, but I think I should tell you about something first."

"What's that?" he asked, continuing the assault with his lips.

"They just made me queen of the Radiants, and I decided to make it so that Elijah and Penelope could be together."

"Well, I suppose congratulations are in order then." Romeo smiled down at her, and it looked almost predatory. It made her feel even more turned on by him, and he took her silence as compliance, scooting her back against the headboard with a sexy growl.

"Well, thank you." She barely got the words out before he began to take her clothes off, ripping his own off at the same time. "But the babies," she laughed and whispered at the same time.

"They're asleep. We'll just have to bite our tongues and be very quiet," he whispered into her ear, his hot breath sending chills down her spine.

-The End-

If you enjoyed this title, I would appreciate your leaving a review of the book. Good reviews encourage an author to write as well as help books to sell. Good reviews can be just a few short sentences describing what you liked about the book without having a spoiler. If you could spend 30 seconds writing a review, I would appreciate it: you can review this title right now at your favorite retailer.

After reading "The Romeo Alpha BBW Paranormal Shifter Romance Series" you can follow your favorite characters twenty-four years later in the "Romeo Alpha Blood Lines Romance Series".

Here is a preview of the **next story** you may enjoy:

Blood Lines: Romeo Alpha Blood Lines Romance, Book 1

ROMEO AND his lovely wife, Amanda, walked the land just outside of their home. Over the last quarter century, they'd purchased hundreds of acres, building on the property borders that Jeremiah, Romeo's father, had purchased before they were born.

"It's lovely this time of day, before the sun wakes."

"It's lovely any morning I get to walk with you," Romeo said, pressing a kiss to Amanda's temple. Neither of them had aged poorly. Romeo was still tall, well-muscled, and ruggedly handsome. His hair, a light brown, was just starting to gray at the temples, making Amanda only more attracted to her sexy husband. He still wore it long, pulling it back into a ponytail because he knew she loved it that way. His blue eyes, still clear and beautiful, smiled at her. "Does that get me brownie points?"

"Only because you're so damned sexy," Amanda grinned. She wore her dark hair pulled into a circle braid and pinned down, knowing full well her husband liked to nuzzle her neck. She liked to let him. "Sarina will become a breeder in two weeks." Amanda didn't need to look at her husband to know his whole body went tense with protectiveness for his oldest daughter.

"I don't want to think about it. I remember what I was like with you. She won't be taking an alpha as a mate and I don't want to talk about it."

"Like it or not, it is something we should discuss. I don't want her brothers thinking that they can keep her under lock and key. We've raised her to be a confident and independent woman."

"And?" Romeo said, hating the logic in his wife's words.

"And, we have to have faith that we raised her right. She's not without her own set of defenses you know," Amanda grinned.

"Yes," Romeo sighed. "Jason, Wade and Joshua."

"More like her powers of witchcraft and her wolf."

"They aren't enough," Romeo growled.

"They'll have to be," Amanda said wisely. "I didn't even know I had powers until my twenty-fourth year. At least she's going into this knowing how it will be for her."

"She's never changed before. With her first full moon coming up, I don't like the idea that all the males in our community will sniff her out."

"We can't keep them away forever, Love. We can, however, continue to give her the tools she needs to choose wisely."

"I didn't let you choose," Romeo said, his blue eyes pensive.

"I don't believe I would have chosen differently, even if I'd been offered someone else as my mate. I was made for you, remember?"

"I'd remember easier if you'd let me have you." Amanda giggled and ran as Romeo got that needy look in his eyes. She loved that look, the one that said simply, *I want you, now*. She played cat and mouse with him for a time before she let him catch her and remind her of what it'd been like when she was twenty-four.

Sarina grinned after besting her twin, Jason, in racquetball. They'd begged and begged their parents for a racquetball court and finally for their eighteenth birthdays, they'd been given their present. The walls were well worn where they'd also played wally ball during inclement weather, when neither the wolves in them, nor their human selves wanted to go outside.

"You just can't win baby brother," Sarina laughed.

"My ass," Jason pouted. *Princess* Sarina never missed an opportunity to rub in the fact that she was older by all of five minutes. "I can best you any time I wish."

"Ha, you can't tell me you let me win every time. Remember brother, we shared the same womb. I know you better than you know yourself."

"Not likely," Jason scoffed. "You have no idea what it's like for me to be with a woman."

Despite the blush that crept along her cheeks, Sarina laughed. "No, but it won't be long now before I find out what it's like to be with a man."

The growl came fast and furious as Jason bared his teeth at the mention of Sarina mating. She'd expected as much and just rolled her eyes. "Ease off J, I haven't taken a man to my bed, yet."

This time when he growled, Sarina grinned when Romeo set a firm hand on his shoulder. "Don't antagonize your brother Sarina. You know he'd rip out the throat of any man who touched you, especially against your will."

"Yes I do, but it's so much fun, Dad."

"Maybe so," Romeo grinned, knowing his two oldest children well. He never told them they were more alike than they were different. Both were fiercely loyal to the other, as well as their family. Both valued the other's opinions, and both would give their lives in protection of their womb-mate, or any member of their family. "But your mother and I appreciate the peace that has finally settled over our house."

Just then, they heard screaming coming from the kitchen. "You were saying?" Amanda giggled. Everyone else followed her into the large kitchen that Romeo had upgraded upon Amanda taking over her Aunt Mabel's mansion. Mabel Walker had been an intensely loyal woman. So loyal in fact that she'd had a hysterectomy to ensure that no wolf would have the say over her breeding rights. She'd let the Walker and Traverse lines and legacies pass on to Amanda, even to the extent of making Amanda believe that she had no other family to care for her after her parents had been killed.

"You son-of-a—"

"I'll thank you not to finish that sentence as I'm the woman who birthed you both," Amanda said, her voice firm.

"Sorry, Mama. But you didn't see what Joshua did!" Shawna whined. At nineteen she was just becoming the woman they'd raised her to be. Still five years off from her own breeding season start, she had much to learn.

"I don't need to see what he did to know that somehow it hurt your feelings."

"She's as sensitive as a new pup," Joshua smirked before getting a thump on the head from his father. "Ow!"

"Tell your sister you're sorry," Romeo warned. "She shared the womb with you, Joshua. Try to remember that when you start bickering and wanting to tease her."

"But she—" Joshua defended himself.

"Whatever you two did to each other doesn't matter now. I can, however, promise that it will matter tonight at supper if you two don't straighten it out."

The twins groaned through their apologies and then went their separate ways. "They're just like you, you know," Amanda chuckled.

"Oh, no. Those two are absolutely yours."

"That they are. I wouldn't have it any other way." Amanda allowed Romeo to pull her into his arms, kissing her soundly. Had it really been nearly twenty-four years since she'd brought their two oldest children into the world? Regardless, the day had been one for their personal history books and he was still just as handsome as she remembered.

Brody Duscene paced back and forth in his home. He could feel the full moon rising, the urge to change gnawing at him ferociously. Panting as it rose high in the sky, he felt the change begin. The searing pain of it ran through his blood and into his bones as they began to lengthen and shift. He bent down to his knees as his hands and feet turned to five-toed paws and his clothes tore away as long, gray fur grew thick over his body.

It always occurred to him after the change that he'd save himself some considerable money if he'd learn to strip before the change, but regardless of the countless times it'd happened since his eighteenth birthday, he had yet to take to the change without his clothes on. The last part to change and always the most painful was his face. His nose lengthened and flattened as his cheek bones and jaw became a muzzle. His tongue grew longer and thinner and his eyes became a keen and sensitive part of his five senses. Within mere minutes he'd become a werewolf and would hunt his prey like a predator, with stealth and a vicious appetite.

Brody waited near a clump of trees as a young couple necked in a car near a stretch of abandoned road. His eyes were barely slits as he watched them. Their soft whispers were easy for his big ears to hear and made the man inside the wolf horny as hell. He always felt guilty when hunting humans, but it was a necessity in order to be a member of Reggie's pack. There were other packs that strictly prohibited the hunting of humans, but switching packs wasn't as easy as changing shirts.

Knowing full well the two love birds in his sights were focused elsewhere, Brody approached the car slowly, sniffing their scents and imprinting them in his memory. If one tried to run, he'd find them. Grabbing the door handle, Brody ripped the door away. He yanked the boy out of the car as the girl screamed. Turning his head back to her, Brody bared his teeth in a snarl that had the girl stumbling away from the car as she attempted to run. Brody let her go, knowing he'd find her when he was done with the boy.

Unlike some in his pack, Brody wasn't one to play with his food. Nor was he the type to hunt with other wolves. He preferred to hunt solo. Whatever he caught was his own. He knew the boundaries of his pack; had been taught them from a pup. But the difference between Brody and the other young wolves in his pack was that Brody *didn't care* about boundaries. Who'd know if he stepped over his section of the world?

Every full moon from the spring equinox, Brody had been exploring regions beyond where his pack lived and hunted. He didn't like hunting in his pack's territory where he'd grown familiar with the local human population. In order to hunt humans he wouldn't get a chance to know, he had to escape the confines Reggie had set for them. Brody was smart enough to know that he wasn't near ready to challenge Reggie for the alpha position of their pack, but soon, very soon, he'd be more than ready.

"Please doggie," the boy in his grip pleaded. The hardest part of the hunt was when his prey begged. Without hesitating much longer, he sank his teeth into the soft flesh of the boy's neck. Blood, rich and full of flavor, rushed past his throat and soaked into his muzzle as he feasted. Brody didn't toy with the humans he preyed upon. Being partly human himself, it always felt like a kick to the teeth to watch another wolf do it, so Brody hunted, ate, and left his carcasses in peace when he was done. He finished the boy with relative ease, licking his lips clean. Returning to the car he picked up the girl's scent and howled at the full moon as he sniffed her out.

Twenty minutes later he found her hovering in the lower branches of an oak tree. He gave her props for being smart enough to climb a tree so he left her there and lay down to sleep. When he woke the next morning naked and sleepy, Brody looked up to see the woman watching him. Smiling, he waved to her before he took off at a sprint. If Reggie caught him outside their boundaries there'd be hell to pay and Brody just wasn't in the mood today.

<<◇>>

"Happy Birthday!"

Sarina heard from everyone as she blew out her birthday candles. Across from her Jason did the same thing. Growing up, they'd always kept the same tradition. Always facing each other and blowing out their candles together as everyone yelled their birthday wishes.

"Can you believe it?" she said to Jason later when their extended family and friends had finally gone home. "We're twenty-four."

"It's just another year, Sis," Jason said, blowing it off and irritating her.

"The hell it is. It's my first breeding year buddy. Just because you don't give a shit, doesn't mean I shouldn't."

"Look, just because you're in an all fire hurry to blow your virginal attributes, doesn't mean that I have to run around as if I've never been laid before."

Sarina snarled at him and stalked off. Finding her mother alone, she sat down on her parent's bed.

"What was it like for you, Mama, when you turned twenty-four?"

"Different from what you're experiencing, I can tell you that," Amanda said as she hung Romeo's dress shirts in the closet. "For starters, when I turned twenty-four I had no idea that I was a werewolf nor a witch. I came to claim my Aunt Mabel's estate and was accosted by your father, who back then was not a people person. He demanded that I marry him and was all too forthcoming with details I didn't want to hear."

"Dad really did that?"

Amanda laughed. "That and more, sweetheart."

"You were a virgin?"

"Yes," Amanda replied. Sarina could tell by the way her mother was eyeing her that she should explain herself.

"I'm nervous," she continued, rushing through the details as if she couldn't breathe. "I don't even have a wolf or man who's interested in me, but I know they will be once they learn I'm in season and especially an alpha's daughter."

"The right man won't care whether you're an alpha's daughter or not. He'll want you for certain, but he'll also care about the woman inside the wolf."

"Did Dad care?"

"In his own way," Amanda smiled. "Like you, we were both young and had less control than we'd probably have liked."

"Is it normal to be scared?"

"Yes," Amanda chuckled. Sarina let her mother pull her into her arms. "Your first time will be something to remember, surely. Just try to remember as well that you don't have to rush. The full moon is nearly a month away and you won't go into season until then. There's still time, especially as werewolves tend to come together in whirlwind circumstances."

"Uncle Elijah and Aunt Penelope didn't," Sarina countered. She knew she was being difficult, but without any prospects and on the day of her twenty-fourth birthday she was feeling edgy.

"Your aunt and uncle certainly did come together in a whirlwind," Amanda explained. "It just so happens that they only thought they couldn't be together. When I became the leading Radiant, I changed the law so that Radiants could marry the loves of their hearts. I didn't want anyone, especially my fellow Radiants, to suffer their hearts for the duties of their souls."

"I hope I'm half the leader you are if it's ever my turn."

"As the oldest, the leadership of the witches would pass to you. However, you could choose to pass it on to Jason if you felt he'd do a better job."

"Not if he doesn't get his head out of his ass," Sarina scoffed.

"And just think. I'd hoped by now you two would have stopped the petty bickering. Aren't there bigger things to worry about?"

"According to him, I'm in an all fired hurry to lose my virginity. Doesn't he know what it's like? Certainly he had a first time too."

"Men rarely see those things the same way as women, darling."

"Still, he could be a little understanding."

"Oh just wait until a man starts sniffing around you. You'll find out how fast your brothers will defend you, even when you wish they wouldn't. Not just Jason either. Wade and Joshua will protect you with the fierceness of our kind. Even Shawna would come to your defense if she was needed."

"Great," Sarina moped. "First I'm a slut, because I want to talk about it. Now I'll have to beat my siblings off the poor man with a stick."

"Who knows, maybe they'll be in the mood to play fetch."

"You always know what to say to make me feel better." Sarina laughed and thanked her mother for the talk.

"It is a skill I learned over time. You will too, darling."

If you enjoyed this sample then look for **Blood Lines: Romeo Alpha Blood Lines Romance, Book 1**.

Here is a preview of **another story** you may enjoy:

Alpha Packed: A BBW Paranormal Shifter Romance - Book 1

THIS WAS a huge mistake. Darlene should have known better, but in utter and total desperation, she agreed to this date. Now the guy in front of her—what was his name again? Steve? Mike? She couldn't even remember now—had been talking non-stop about pro wrestling. But not even actual real wrestling. The stuff that was fake and basically just soap operas with some terrible phony fights thrown in.

"So then the Ice Cube challenged The Man to a battle!"

"Wow, really?" Darlene replied, feigning interest on every possible level.

This was her mistake. She had been spending way too much time at home lately, curled up on the couch, binge watching reality television shows because they made her feel better about her boring life. Darlene would leave for work in the mornings, do eight hours at a boring local bookstore, come home, eat and watch TV. She also stayed up far later than any normal human should, which resulted in limited forms of social communication.

That was how Darlene ended up on some free dating website. She deleted most of the messages she got. They were mostly from guys who seemed to think of her as a sexual fetish instead of an actual human being. Getting messages from guys who were into her being overweight made her feel uncomfortable. Darlene either got disgusted looks or sexual lust over her size.

Both sucked. She had been about to delete her page for good when a guy who appeared to be normal messaged her. He hadn't made any gross comments about her size and even made her laugh once or twice with his messages. It had been eight months since her last relationship blew up in her face. *Why not try something different?* She decided to accept his date.

The guy was so boring that Darlene wished the restaurant would go up in flames so she could flee. She was flipping through her options on how to end the date early when he finally pushed his plate away.

"That was delicious," he said.

"Oh yeah. It was great," Darlene lied, thinking the potatoes were too dry for her liking.

The check came and the guy—what was his name!—made an effort to search for his wallet. *Oh here we go...*

"Oh man. I forgot my wallet at home!" he said with fake surprise.

"Yeah, yeah, I got it," she mumbled, slamming her debit card on the table.

It didn't take a genius to figure out this asshole had asked her out to throw her what he thought was a "pity date" and get a free meal out of her. He would probably go home to all his idiot friends and talk about how he gave the fat girl a date because he was just so nice. Darlene felt like punching him in the face.

She paid, and they walked out of the restaurant in silence. He escorted her to her car and then glanced around, as if checking so that no one could see him, before he tried to kiss her.

"Yeah," Darlene lifted up her hand to block him, "I don't think so. Thanks for nothing though, seriously."

The man scowled and before he could say something back, Darlene got into her car. She pulled out of the parking lot as quickly as she could, wanting to forget the entire terrible date.

What a mistake. What an absolute mistake. Not even just the date. The last couple years of her life had been a huge mistake. She wished she could travel back in time and re-do everything. The first thing she'd do would be to say a resounding *no* when Austin proposed to her.

Darlene pulled into her apartment complex five minutes later. She had picked a nearby restaurant so she could make a quick escape home if needed. She walked up to the second floor. The couple by the stairwell was fighting again. They were constantly screaming at each other over everything. Some nights, Darlene wanted to yell back at them to just break up. Other times, she wanted to tell them to make it work, because being alone was terrible.

She opened the front door of her apartment and glanced around. Her computer was on in one corner, and a few blankets were thrown on the couch for maximum comfort for those times when she drowned herself in ice cream and terrible reality shows.

Everything else was clean though. Darlene couldn't stand her apartment being messy or dirty. She wanted it to be perfect, as if she could make her apartment look like how she didn't feel.

Darlene yanked off her high heels and plopped down in front of her computer. She deleted the online dating profile and stared out the window. That was it — she was going to become a hermit. Well, as much of a hermit as one can be if they still had to go to work and grocery shop and run errands…but other than that she was totally going to be a hermit from now on. People were not her thing. People were just terrible all around. And she'd had enough of terrible people.

She moved to the couch, wrapping herself up in a blanket. Darlene mused over what she would watch. Terrible shows about being tricked into online dating seemed like a good end to the night. It'd make her feel better at the very least.

Her cellphone rang loudly. Darlene jolted awake, startled. She wasn't used to her new ringtone. It used to be the theme song of an old cartoon she liked, but after everything went to hell she changed it to a normal ring in an effort to seem more adult. Now the ring was bleating loudly and annoying her. She looked at the front of the screen… her boss.

"Hello?"

"Hey, sorry, did I wake you?"

"No, Maria," Darlene lied. "What's up?"

"I had to fire Jacob. Can you cover his shift? You'd be working till three."

Darlene glanced at the clock to see it was a little past eight in the morning. "That's fine. I'll leave now."

She hopped in the shower, letting the warm water rush over her. She wasn't surprised that Maria had to fire Jacob. He was constantly late and unable to help any of the customers who came into the shop. The bookstore was small and dealt with books that couldn't be found at any of the chains. Business was slow, but the books were rare enough that Maria only needed to sell a few each month to keep the business going. Darlene liked how quiet it was and the fact that human interaction was minimal. She knew she needed to get over this slump she was in, but felt no desire to. Almost everything Darlene did as of late seemed to feed into it — her lifestyle, her job, even the stupid things she spent time watching and looking up online.

The bookstore was only a ten-minute drive to downtown and located between a coffee shop and a cheesy massage parlor. Maria hated the massage parlor. She thought it was tacky and ruined the charm of the street. Darlene usually liked to watch to see how many guys went in there. She swore it was a front for some hookers.

Darlene parked her car and headed toward the bookshop. She could already tell no one was in the store. She walked inside and waved to Maria.

"Oh, I am so glad you are here!" Maria exclaimed when she saw Darlene. "I'll have to hire someone right away, but you and I will have to work extra in the meantime."

"No problem," Darlene replied, shoving her purse under the front counter.

Darlene worked here for almost four years. Maria was a good boss. She always treated Darlene with respect and even gave her an entire month off after her father passed away three years ago. She was an older Native American woman with a bushy head of white hair that she barely cared enough to run a comb through. She wore large glasses that looked like they were from the seventies. Her fashion left a lot to be desired. Maria seemed to put on whatever she grabbed first and didn't look twice in the mirror afterward. For instance, today she had on a blue shirt with an off-color green skirt and black shoes. Her earrings were painted octopuses she had probably made herself — she liked making crazy jewelry.

"So," Darlene asked. "What happened with Jacob?"

Maria scowled. "He comes into work high as a kite, stinking of weed. Starts rambling to me about how he was in the woods last night and *like, totally felt something, like, man*," Maria said, mimicking Jacob's slow tone. "He was an hour late on top of it. I can't have someone late, stinking of weed and scaring off the few customers I get each month… especially after the last incident."

"Yeah, that was a mess." Jacob had hit on one of their regular clients in such a crass manner that she had threatened never to return again.

"Anyway, thank you so much for covering. I'm going to head off now. One of the grandkids is having a birthday party. You'll be okay?"

Darlene cast a sarcastic glance around the empty bookstore. "Wow, I hope I can handle it."

Maria laughed and grabbed her purse, heading to the door before stopping. "Hey, how was your date?"

Darlene frowned. "A total mess."

"Sorry, love. Hang in there, okay?" Maria said before leaving.

Hang in there. Darlene sighed. She has been hanging in there for way too long. When was she going to get a grip on her own life again? She walked around the shop to make sure everything was in its proper place. Darlene knew it would be, of course. It wasn't as if they had a ton of customers come through.

Maria had the marketable books up front, which brought in some tourist traffic during the summer. The farther back in the store one went, the stranger the books became. Darlene ended up in the back again, like she always did. Maria kept the supernatural books back here — books about ghosts, werewolves, mermaids and all sorts of paranormal creatures. Darlene always felt drawn to these; she never knew why. As a kid, she liked to pretend to be a ghost hunter. Nowadays, she liked to watch terrible B-movies about ghosts.

She trailed her fingers along the spines, letting the musty old-book smell wash over her. Darlene stopped in front of one book about ghosts, pulling it off the shelf. She had just flipped it open to a random page when the tiny bell on the door jingled. Surprised, Darlene looked up.

A tall man in amazing shape walked in. He had brown eyes, a beard and scruffy hair and wore a leather jacket. Darlene found herself gawking at him. He was so handsome her knees turned to jelly.

"Hi!" she said, but her voice sounded too high pitched, like she was eleven. "Hi, sorry, back here." She walked up front to him.

"Hello," he said in a deep voice that sent shivers down her back.

"Hi," Darlene repeated and then tried to get a hold of herself. "How can I help you?"

"I'm lost. I'm trying to find Roman's Tavern."

Her eyes widened. "I don't know if it's open yet."

Was this guy a hardcore alcoholic? It was still early in the morning, and he wanted to find a bar. Roman's Tavern was the only bar in town that Darlene hadn't ever gone to. It brought in a wild crowd that made her uneasy. Any time she drove past it and saw the crazy partying in there, she realized how much she wanted to go and that scared her. She was never much of a partier.

The fact that such an overwhelming urge to go when she drove by made her nervous. What if she went and lost her head?

The cops were there often, breaking up fights. Bike gangs were always seen there. Sometimes, if she left work at closing time, she'd drive by it and hear the thumping music and smell the cigarette smoke. She thought about going in every time. What would happen? Would she get hurt? What if she was missing out on something?

To Darlene, Roman's Tavern represented a life she could jump into if only she wasn't afraid. But she *was* too afraid. Life as a hermit was too comforting.

"Do you know where I can find it anyway?" he asked.

"It's down the street. On the corner, kind of pushed back a bit. It has this rundown broken sign that you might see if you drive by it."

"Thanks a lot, Miss…"

"Darlene." She held out her hand.

He stared at it for a second and then shook it. "Idris. Thanks for the help. You guys sell books about ghosts?" He pointed to the book she was holding when he came in.

His hand was so warm that Darlene had to snap herself back to the conversation. Was he sick? Shouldn't he be resting instead of going to some bar?

"Yes," she managed to respond. "We have a supernatural section in the back. Ghosts, vampires, werewolves…the usual."

"Werewolves, huh?" he replied. "Okay, well, nice to meet you."

Before Darlene could say anything else, he was gone.

She stood there, clutching her book to her chest, thinking about the feeling of warmth from his hand. What in the world was that about?

If you enjoyed this sample then look for **Alpha Packed: A BBW Paranormal Shifter Romance - Book 1**.

Here is a preview of **another story** you may enjoy:

Devil's Advocate: A BBW MC New Adult Romance Series - Book 4 by Carla Coxwell

KRISTIE MISSED her own bed. It felt like ages since she slept in it. In reality, it had only been three days. She tried telling herself that as she stared up at the hospital ceiling. She ran her fingers over her baby bump. *Not long now*, she thought to herself as she waited for the doctor. But it would be a dangerous final two months until the baby was born.

Severe morning sickness. What was the fancy name the doctor had for it all those months ago? *Hyperemesis Gravidarum.* Kristie could never remember the exact name. All it meant to her was that the violent vomiting she experienced early on wasn't the typical morning sickness. It increased as she got farther along in her pregnancy. She had a particular nasty bout of it this week. Gray begged her to go to the hospital, for the baby's sake so Kristie finally relented.

It was a good thing she did. She was extremely dehydrated. Now she was waiting to hear if she could be released today. Gray said he would be by soon with Megan. He had been to see her this morning but had to go to work.

Kristie closed her eyes, suddenly missing Megan, who was growing so rapidly. It felt like just yesterday that they had taken her in after Kass and Rick were murdered. At the thought of her best friend, Kristie felt a pang in her chest. Her best friend, gunned down by the Infernos, leaving only Megan alive.

Taking in Megan was unexpected. Both Kristie and Gray struggled when they became parents. They had barely taken in Megan when Kristie found out the impossible had happened – she was pregnant. She had given up hope of having a child of her own and had decided that she would focus fully on Megan. The next thing she knew, she was pregnant, vomiting over a toilet bowl while Gray tried to take care of Megan.

Gray handled the news perfectly. For some reason, Kristie was completely terrified that he would be enraged at her pregnancy. They had just taken Megan in and Gray had lost his best friend. But he was overjoyed at the news and slowly, over the course of her pregnancy, he began to change.

In fact, everything would be perfect if it weren't for the Infernos. But wasn't that always the case? Kristie had noticed a shift in Gray, as if he was finally backing away from the gang. But the tendrils of that life refused to fully release Gray. Sometimes Kristie would wake up, having to pee several times a night, and he would be in Megan's room, watching her sleep, lost in thought.

Breaking through her thoughts, the doctor came in to tell her she was going to be released today. Relieved, Kristie called Gray.

"Thanks for watching her the past few days."

"No problem," Lionel replied, handing Megan over to Gray. "I'm glad we could help."

"I'll have Kristie call Pamela once she gets home."

Lionel nodded and gave a small wave as Gray juggled Megan and all of her things toward the truck. She was fast asleep. She could sleep almost anywhere. Gray envied her as he put her in her car seat. She gave out a soft noise and settled back into her slumber.

Gray got into the driver's seat and headed toward the hospital. He was glad Kristie was coming home. He knew she was going stir crazy in the hospital. He remembered his own time in the hospital and could relate. Being pregnant on top of that must make it even worse.

It was silly but Gray still hadn't fully wrapped his mind around the fact that Kristie was pregnant. It seemed almost unreal to him. They tried for months but there was nothing. Now a baby boy was on the way in two months. Gray glanced back at Megan while stopped at a red light. She was sleeping soundly. She was the perfect mix of Kass and Rick.

His mood turned dark at the thought of his best friend. Gone from this world, struck down by the Infernos. Gray swore revenge for everything Armand had done – shooting Kristie, killing Rick and Kass and leaving Megan an orphan. But the urge for revenge began to fade. With Kristie pregnant and Megan under their care, it seemed selfish to drag out the violence any longer than he already had. If he died, what would happen to Kristie and their two children? Rick had realized he was growing up and was trying to leave the life as well. It seemed foolish not to go.

But leaving the gang was harder than it looked. Even if Gray pulled out of the group and stopped interacting with them, Armand and the Infernos wouldn't let him leave. They would still track him down and hurt him. It was a personal grudge now. They would either kill him or make sure he went to jail for the rest of his life.

So Gray found himself stuck between trying to settle down as a family man and trying to detangle himself from gang life. Kristie had been stressing the importance of communication to him, as if Gray could simply invite Armand out for a cup of tea and settle everything that way.

He pulled into the hospital parking lot. The hospital held such terrible memories for him. He hoped Kristie's pregnancy would offer him something good for a change. He put Megan into her carrier and headed up to get Kristie.

She sat upright in bed. The TV was on some daytime judge show, but her eyes were glazed over from boredom. Her skin was pale, as it had been since her violent morning sickness began. But when Kristie saw him, her eyes lit up.

"Hey," he whispered, pointing to the sleeping Megan.

She nodded and gave a small wave. The discharge procedure took forever and by the time they wheeled Kristie out in her wheelchair, Megan had awakened and was fussing loudly.

"My mom called me right before you came into the room," Kristie said as they headed home. "She wants to come over and help make dinner in the next couple of days. To see how I'm doing."

Gray made a non-committal noise. Things had only mildly improved after they adopted Megan. Pamela, Kristie's mother, wasn't thrilled upon hearing Kristie was pregnant. It made things incredibly awkward for Gray. His uncle was still hung up over the fact Kristie and Gray were cousins. Pamela still blamed him for Kristie's shooting. She was hoping her daughter would divorce him. Being pregnant wasn't part of the plan.

"I think they want to spend more time with Megan," Kristie was saying, not noticing Gray's face. "I said it was fine. Of course I had to say it was fine."

"I understand. They're her grandparents. They'd want to see her."

Kristie nodded, although her facial expression told Gray all he needed to know. She understood how awkward it was for everyone involved.

They arrived home. January snow fell gently. Gray made sure Megan was warm and snug before taking her out of the truck. They headed toward their apartment. Gray thought that even though Kristie had just gotten out of the hospital, she still looked beautiful.

They had moved again. This time to the complex where Rick and Kass used to live. Kass's parents and Gray's own uncle helped out with the rent each month. His uncle said that Pamela helped out as well, but Gray wasn't so sure about that. In any case, with people pitching in to help pay for a bigger apartment, it meant they were able to live in an apartment complex with much better security. It had two bedrooms, unlike their last apartment where Megan's room was non-existent. It was all enclosed which made Kristie feel safer, and was nicer than their last place.

They stepped inside and Kristie scooped up Megan, who badly needed a diaper change and a feeding. Gray offered to help but his words were lost on Kristie, who was giggling and cooing over Megan as usual.

As he watched Kristie tend to Megan and looked around their new apartment, he thought everything had a shot at being perfect. He just had to get out of the Devil's Advocates.

If you enjoyed this sample then look for **Devil's Advocate: A BBW MC New Adult Romance Series - Book 4 by Carla Coxwell**.

Other Books by Darla Dunbar

- Romeo Alpha Blood Lines Romance Series (This series follows "The Romeo Alpha BBW Paranormal Shifter Romance Series")

- The Alpha Feud BBW Paranormal Shifter Romance Series

- The Alpha Packed BBW Paranormal Shifter Romance Series

- The Daemon Paranormal Romance Chronicles

- The Mind Talker Paranormal Romance Series

- The Leather Satchel Paranormal Romance Series

Get the latest update on new releases from the author at:

https://darladunbar.com/newsletter/

About the Author - Darla Dunbar

Darla has been interested in paranormal romance since she was a teenager in high school. It was then that she discovered she could fulfill her fantasies through her writing.

Observing people and human behavior in the area of romance has always been one of her favorite pastimes. Combining that with an overactive imagination is a sure fire way of coming up with interesting themes.

Connect with Darla Dunbar

I really appreciate you reading my book! Here are my social media coordinates:

Friend me on Facebook:
https://www.facebook.com/darladunbar/

Follow me on Twitter: https://twitter.com/DarlDunbar

Check me out on Goodreads:
https://www.goodreads.com/author/show/8425857.Darl a_Dunbar

Subscribe to my newsletter:
https://darladunbar.com/newsletter/

Visit my website: https://darladunbar.com/